# THE
# LAND OF A
# HUNDRED
# SPIRITS

# THE LAND OF A HUNDRED SPIRITS

## ANYANWU TIMOTHY CHIBUIKE

Abibiman
Publishing

New York & London

First published in the United Kingdom in 2024
by Abibiman Publishing
www.abibimanpublishing.com

Abibiman Publishing is registered under Hudics LLC
in the United States and in the United Kingdom

ISBN: 978-1-7395395-9-7

Cover design by Fred Martins

Printed at Clays UK

# CONTENTS

## CHAPTER ONE

# ODU MARRIAGE AND THE FATHERHOOD

**ODU WAS** naked as they journeyed. The Dibia had painted him with Nzu. In between his lips was a strand of Omu that was tied on both edges. The rest of his body was adorned with ijenwangbada. On his head was a smoking abubu in a clay pot. The distance between him and the other villagers was about twenty metres. It was only the Dibia, Eze-Amadioha and a few traditionalists in Umuagba that were close to him. Far behind the elders was Odu's wife, Obiageri. She had two kids and was seven months old pregnant. From the way she was walking, one could know that she was behind others not because she had so wished or because the elders were stronger than her, but because the tradition demanded that. Eze-amadioha had earlier told her to stay at home or like other women, go to her Umunna, but she insisted that she would be beside her husband to the end.

It was a freezing day, but because of the long distance already covered, everyone was sweating. Their feet must have regretted having known that day as they trod from slightly wet to a very dampy soil, from a plain ground to a hilly one. They had also passed through the thorny land of Onu-acha, and were then heading to Ihuala where everything would take place. It has been a lonely track road; none talked to the other nor looked back. The only sound that could be heard was that of chipping birds.

Back in Umuagba village, everywhere looked like a cemetery. All huts were shut because the elders warned their children not to come out throughout the day. No married woman was in Umuagba village that day because women were not permitted to be in a village when such omenala was done, except in certain cases where the wife of the man in question may be allowed. As a matter of fact, women used the previous evening to run to their various homes with their grown up daughters. In every household, it was only boys that have not done Iwa-akwa initiation, and girls under the age of fifteen that could be seen. All expectations were to hear the news of what fate awaited Odu.

After a long tiring journey, they reached Ihuala. The shrine was a very fearful one. The effigies of the gods were all decorated with Omu, red clothing and blood of a he-goat that was earlier killed in Odu's compound. The he-goat was brought by Eze-amadioha together with a tortoise, lizard, two black pigeons, five red candles, four kola nuts that represented the four market days in Igboland, and a keg of undiluted palm wine. Before they left the village, the slaughtered he-goat, life tortoise, two out of the five candles, and a pigeon were buried in the middle of Obiama. The Dibia then went closer to the effigies and made some incantations. In a moment, everywhere was filled up with an offensive odour. There was dead silence for about five minutes. Then Eze-amadioha went closer, dipped his hand into his bag, brought out the kola nut, and the remaining three sticks of candles and handed them over to the Dibia who was holding the pigeon and lizard. The lizard and the pigeon were strangled before the shrine. Another moment of uncomfortable silence was broken by lightening accompanied with a deafening thunder. As the thunder roared, the sacrifices that were earlier buried before the journey started appeared before the shrine. Eze-Amadioha then bade Odu to come closer. For the second time, he dipped his hand into his bag and brought out an Ofo, dipped it into the sacrifice that had earlier appeared and gave it to Odu. Immediately Odu received the Ofo, there was total darkness accompanied with intermittent lightening. Odu swung the ofo around his head six times and at the seventh time, he fell down. "Ewooo!, chim egbuo muooo, Nwodu odikwa ndu…

biko nu, dim odi kwa ndu?" These words broke the silence that lasted for more than three hours. Obiageri uttered those words when she saw her husband lying on the ground.

The Dibia was annoyed. Obiageri had unintentionally broken the communication between the gods and the Dibia. That meant that the ritual must be repeated before everything could work out again. Eze-Amadioha signaled as if he was saying the Dibia should not worry. He dipped his hand into his bag for the third time, brought out powder-like substance, blew it into the air and everything was normalized. Immediately Odu stood up after sneezing three times. Eze-Amadioha then bade Kwendu and Obilo to come. They joined Odu where he was sitting when Eze-amadioha mixed a concoction of blood and Nzu, broke the kola nuts into particles and presented them before the three men involved. Odu was the first to take the kolanut, dip it into the oku that was filled with the concoction and ate. Kwendu and Obilo followed suit. The whole elders present were then served with the meal of oji and concoction. Everyone except Obiageri ate the concoction.

All roads led to the village square when the ritual was over, with everyone building an expectation. Unlike when they were going, Odu was wearing his clothes. He was like every other villager, but he could not talk to anyone. He was very weak and was wanting in strength to continue his journey back home. So even if anyone was willing to talk to him, he hadn't energy to reply. No one knew what fate awaited him. But from the look of things, everyone except Obiageri, Ebo and Ezeala was praying for Odu not to survive the oath. When they got to the Obiama, there was deadly silence everywhere, but this was soon broken by the roar of four Mkpo-nala shots before everyone left.

It was night, although to the youths of Umuagba, there was nothing like day that day. They had all been indoors sleeping. Everywhere was quiet. People had prepared and taken their dinner and had gone to bed very early. That night knew no light from the heavenlies; it was as if God has never said, "let there be light". The only iota of light that one could manage to see was coming from Obiama, which was the handiwork of the Dibia. That was the light that Odu had earlier carried to the shrine. Immediately it was 8:30pm, a heavy rain came from nowhere. It rained with lightening throughout the night. No one had experienced such rain fall and thunder that roared that night. At each of the thunder storms, everyone would think that Odu was the one that the heavenlies were searching for. "That thunder was exactly Amadioha", one would say in his house. At about 10am the following day, everyone was still in his room though it had stopped raining. It was around 11am that people started coming out from their houses.

From that very day, Odu and his wife were nothing but indigenous strangers. The only bond they had with the people of Umuagba was that they walked on the same road. Life was not friendly with them. To make the matter worst, Odu never slept for a night without terrible nightmares. Most times, he would dream of masquerades chasing him. One morning, he narrated to his wife how he was being chased by a masquerade the previous night. According to him, the masquerade was holding casket on one hand and a parcel of land on the other hand. At some point in the dream, the masquerade would grow taller than an electric pole and at some other times, it would look like a dwarf. As the masquerade was chasing him, he ran into his father's room and woke his father who then threw nkwu-ojukwu on the masquerade before it left. Immediately after that, his father took him to strategic places in their compound and told him to dig out some things buried in those places. His father also told him to be very strong as there were many other deadlier masquerades coming his way.

When Odu woke that very day, it was raining heavily. As he stepped out of his room, the first thing he saw was a dead bat. It was indeed a bad omen. What brought a bat to my house? He asked rhetorically. At the other corner of the house was a piece of red cloth tied round a basket containing four eggs. It was at this point that Odu remembered the places his father showed him in his dreams the previous night. He then moved around his compound and saw all manner of strange things. He was indeed frightened by all these. He quickly locked the door from outside so that his wife would not come out and see those strange things. He then walked straight to his father's tomb and made some statements seeking for his father's protection and accompaniment. After that, he walked straight to those points, picked the strange things with his left hand and took them to Oke-Acha stream where he disposed them.

Since that day, such occurrence became a routine in Odu's house. There would always be such things every morning. One morning, his wife saw him. She had been suspecting that her husband has been hiding something from her. That morning, Odu came out as usual to cleanse the compound. But standing in the center of his compound was his dead mother who was holding a pestle and a matchet. As soon as she saw Odu, tears rolled down her cheeks. She then walked straight to Odu who felt he was in a trance. Immediately, she raised the pestle to strike him; his father appeared and held her by her hands. He started scolding the wife for being so cheap to be bribed and influenced to kill her own son. As all these things were happening, Odu was standing without making any move. He didn't know that the wife was monitoring him in bewilderment. When Obiageri realized that all was not well was when Odu began to run round his house screaming and muttering unintelligible things. All these got Obiageri afraid. She concluded that her husband has gone mad. Luckily, within few minutes, everything subsided. Odu was surprised to see Obiageri standing outside instead of being in the bedroom. As he walked towards his wife, Obiageri kept moving backwards avoiding his attempt to touch her. It was when Odu called her by her pet name - 'Oby Nkem' that she succumbed.

That day was a day of story and mystery for Obiageri. Odu narrated all that had happened since the day he swore the Amadioha. "Ole kwanu nke butere ina-agbaghari ulo gburu-gburu n'ututu a", asked Obiageri. Odu explained that it was when his mother was determined to strike him with a pestle and machete that his dead father rebuked and chased her round the compound to seize those weapons from her. My father had claimed that my uncle invoked the spirit of my dead mother and armed her to kill me because they have tried so many means to no avail.

Two months after the incident at Ihuala, Obiageri was seen one sunny Monday afternoon. It was on 10th of July, 1989. She was carrying one of her sons at her back. The other one who was about three years old was walking beside her. The third child was in her womb for the past nine months. They were struggling to get over Umuagba hill: a very rough and high hill. One does not need to be told that she has known agony since last night. She was beginning to undergo the peril of labour. "Bia nwam, why are you stressing yourself like this, you are pregnant…was there no one at home to leave these kids for…? These were questions thrown to Obiageri by one Umueze palm wine tapper who had seen her state that afternoon. It was not as if Obiageri liked suffering herself. The truth of the matter was that there was no one to leave the children with. Her husband went to the farm since the past three days. And since the incident of the two months ago, no villager was rapporting with Odu's family. This was not according to Eze-Amadioha's instruction though; they had decided to take part with Odu's rivals to make life miserable for him and his family. Odu could not be welcomed in anyone's house; his children and wife were not exempted. Everyone had warned their children to have nothing to do with Odu's children. This was the circumstance that led Obiageri to carry her two kids along with her wherever she went.

Not sooner she got to the maternity home, than 20minutes, Odu appeared. It was like a magic for her because it was not the day she was expecting her husband to return from the farm. Having gone to the farm three days before, it was expected that Odu would return in the next four days. She was happy, but could not say any word to him because of the pains she was passing through. Before long, she was led to the labour room where she delivered within one hour of her entrance. It was a male child. Odu was the happiest man on earth. He then had three sons. At least, if Amadioha strikes him, he had hoped that someone would succeed him. Out of joy, a thought and a name came up to him; he decided that during naming ceremony of his son, he would give him the name Ogumka. and that he would raise the boy to be a religious person. These he said because Amadioha has proven that his hands were clean. Joyfully, Odu bailed his wife out after a day of her delivery.

    Hahahaeee, ogha ogho-gho, chineke imena ooo!

        Unu muru nwa gini eee?!

        Nwa nwoke ooo

        Eji gini azu ya ee!?

        Ihe eriwere enye nwa e, enye nwa e, enye nwae

        Eriwe ji enye nwa, eriwe ede enye nwa

        Tiho tiho, anyi nwe ebea nwe ebea!

These were the words of the jubilation that was coming out from Odu's compound. It was his ndi ogo that were making the joyful noise. The news of the safe delivery had reached Umuoka, Obigeri's native village. Knowing the nature of things in Umuagba, they all knew that Odu and his wife would feel more dejected if no one celebrates with them, so they made it mandatory that everyone had to go to Umuagba to celebrate with their inlaw. Like what they expected, no Umuagba villager had visited nor had congratulated Odu for his fortune. Instead, his compound was as quiet as a burial ground.

    Some months had passed. Isinna was puzzled as to why him and his brother Ezeji were being treated unfairly by his peers. He had wanted to ask his father all these while, but he thought it was never daddy's business. After all, dad don't play with them, so how was he supposed to know what was going on between him and his peers. But one day, Isinna decided to find out what the root of the problem was. It was a day he went for moon light play, all the children were playing but never allowed Isinna and Ezeji to join them. At a point, papa Udo summoned the children for a season of folktale. But the old man ordered the two brothers out before he started his story telling. As a matter of fact, Isinna decided that whatever be the cause of the isolation, dad must know. So he would tell him that night.

When they got home, dad and mum had already gone to bed. He thought for a while, and later went to bed too. That night, he could not sleep. He had done everything he thought could induce him to sleep, but to no avail. All he was thinking was his plight. At around 12:30am, his puzzle became so haunting that he decided to go and wake his father. He went to his father's room, and to his greatest surprise, his father was not sleeping. Odu was also thinking about his plight. He had lived a life of isolation for a while and thus was disturb by such life. "Isinna what are you still doing by this time of the night? You supposed to be sleeping by now. Are you alright? He asked in pretense; for he knew that Isinna had been awake till then. But he was not very sure what could make a boy in his age to still remain awake till then. "Why should I sleep father? Were you not the one that told me that great men don't sleep when others are sleeping? You also told me that wise and courageous men conquer their problems before closing their eyes in bed". His father was surprised that his six years old son could remember to put what he told him three months ago to work. "Bia nwam, ole ihe bu nsogbu gi?". Isinna was happy when his father gave him the attention he needed. He therefore decided not to misuse the opportunity. "Nnam, I have been dying in silence for a while, I don't like the way Ezeji and I are being treated by our peers. They don't associate with us; they always keep us away from everything they do. Even some elders don't respond to our greetings whenever we greet them. But the one that made me not to sleep this night was the one done by Papa Udo. We were in the village square when he summoned all the children to tell us stories. When I went with my brother, he ordered us out. This made the other children to laugh at us so mockingly. Please dad tell me if you know what my brother and I have done to the villagers"

Odu breathed heavily when he heard the pathetic experience of his poor son, but it was too early to tell him the root of the matter. On a second thought, he felt he should do that because the lad had proven his mental maturity. He never expected him to be so disturbed by the way things were going not to talk of having a sleepless night over it. "my son" he called

"I had believed that I would tell you the root of the matter one day, but I had not believed that it would be this early. Since you have asked, I cannot restrain myself from telling you what you have asked for. It all started last eight years; in 1986 when my father died. Before then, I had been in good terms with my uncles in particular and the villagers in general. But after the death, things started changing gradually. I had buried my father as a hero which he was and had inherited all he had as his only surviving son. Few months had passed, and I wanted to travel back to Kaduna- the place I was staying. Because of the enormous expenses I made during the burial, I had no money to travel with. This prompted me to sell a portion of my land to raise the needed money. I gave your mother some cash to start up a business and to take care of the family. Having kept everywhere in order, I decided to travel on Monday that followed. On Sunday that would predate my travelling date, I had gone to bed on time. Around 8pm, your mother woke me up, and told me that my uncle, Kwendu visited and wanted to see me with no delay. I was happy when she told me that because I saw that as an opportunity to have blessing from my uncle before travelling the following day. I greeted him when I met him, instructed your mother to get me kola nut to serve him". "Excuse me dad, why did you have to offer him kola nut, since he was always with you and by extension, you had taken him for a father?" interrupted Isinna. I had to offer him kola nut because courtesy demanded that I should do so. Besides, that I took him as a father does not mean that I lived in the same house with him. So having visited my house, I owe him kola nut".

"He told me not to worry about kola as what he came for did not call for it. I then sat with all ease, for him to say what his visit was for. He asked me if I knew anything about the land at okpotoro-ulo which one Mr. Eke was then working on. Yes, I replied and told him that I was the one that sold the land to him. I also seized the opportunity and pleaded with him for not informing him before selling the land. Although I didn't have to do that; after all, it was my land. He rebuked me, and claimed ownership of the land. I was surprised to hear him say the land belonged to him. I then asked him the exact land he was talking about because by saying the land was his own, I believed we were not discussing a particular land. But when he gave me the description and location of the land he was talking about; it was exactly the one I was also talking about. 'But uncle I had farmed on the land with my dad when he was alive and he told me that the land belongs to us. Even my mother had also listed all my lands for me and was aware that I sold the land to make up with my transport fare and settle other expenses I made during my father's burial. He then stood up, called me, and told me to either give him the money I realized from the land or tell Mr. Eketo stay away from the land. As soon as he said this, he left.

I was disturbed by this and immediately called my mother and informed her about the development and sought that she tell me more about the land. She replied that she had nothing more to tell me apart from what I already know about the land. And that the land is mine by inheritance. That night, I was more disturbed than you are this night. I thought of what I would do the following morning before travelling, but could not arrive at anything. If I had to travel, who knows what may come up later. On the other hand, how can I stay back from a planed journey because of an issue that may worth less. I was very confused that night. I never wanted to tell your mother, but I could not help myself. I finally opened up to her. She advised me not to travel then, that I should rather wait till the next three days, by then, everything would have been settled. I adhered to her instruction, but was restless that night.

Early the following morning, I had a knock on my door. It was Mr. Eke. He reiterated how he was warned by my uncle last night not to enter into that farmland again unless he wished to die. He was highly disturbed by the threat because my uncle, Kwendu, was not known for making empty threats. I told him not to worry, and promised to settle the differences amicably. Immediately, I ran to the farmland in question and discovered that it has been surrounded with Omu and ogugu. The implication was that nobody was expected to enter into the land, not to talk of working in it. I was furious at the sight of this. I went straight to my uncle's house and asked him why he had done that. He told me that what he did was in his land, and that what he did there was no one's business.

When I realized that the tone of the pipe had changed, I went to the village head and reported to him. He promised that he would summon my uncle before noon and would relay whatever he discussed with him to me immediately. Around 3pm, I was summoned by the Eze, he told me that he had met with my uncle and that he was seriously laying claims to that particular land, with another four of my farmlands. I was dumbfounded at this. I never believed that my uncle could be the one to frustrate me. He never came when my father was still alive. I inquire from the Eze about the remaining portions of land which he was claiming too, but seeing how furious I was, he calmed me down and promised to settle the case amicably. I went home that evening with anger. It was then obvious to me that my journey would not take place in the next one month or even two.

Around 7:45pm, I was at home that day when the Eze's messenger came to me and reported that the Eze would want to see me the following day around 10am. Before 9:30, I was at the palace. Within a while, my uncle arrived. The Eze was the last to come out. We stood and greeted him. He ordered us to sit. He served us kola nut and then said the reason he had summoned us. He gave me the room to explain what I had complained to him the previous day, and I reiterated my story. He then asked uncle Kwendu if he had something to say. Uncle

Kwendu told him that the land I sold was his own and that I was still possessing some other portions of his land. The Eze asked us if we both had evidences to the ownership of the lands in question. "Yes I have" replied both of us. He then rescheduled the meeting two days later and bid each of us to come with a plate of Ugba prepared with ukwu-ewu, four kola nuts each and a jar of palm wine.

It was then that it became obvious to me that I had entered a case that would last for more than a year with my uncle. Having a case with the king and his cabinets was an ordeal anyone would not like to have. It was time consuming and expensive. Most times, it was not the truth that justifies the winner, rather the ability to influence the Eze and his cabinet. As I reached home, I gathered every evidence I had pertaining my ownership to all my lands. I put them in a particular box while selecting those that had to do with the disputed lands. When I was having a discussion with your mother, she suggested that I should let go of the land instead of having a long lasting feud with my uncle. Although I rebuked her, I later decided to adopt her advice. Before the scheduled date, I had gathered the money that I realized from the land I sold to Mr. Eke. I wanted to give it to my uncle as he had earlier requested so that there would be peace between us. Besides, I felt it was too early for me to stay in the village to drag land with old men.

It was Afo market day, your mother had prepared the Ugba, and I took it with other things listed by the Eze to the palace. I then had to run home to get my evidence of ownership to the disputed land which I had forgotten. On my way to the palace with the papers, I was ambushed. Though I was not touched, the papers were snatched from me. The men had taken both the papers and the money I had earlier budgeted to give my uncle. It was hell for me because I knew with the particulars, it would be difficult for me to win the case, not to talk of now that the papers were no more. I stood confused for some minutes thinking of what next to do, but nothing came up to me. I then proceeded to the palace. Before my arrival, the whole palace was filled with the council of elders, and it was as if they were all waiting for me. When I walked in without anything, I noticed that my uncle was putting up a smile. I then realized he has hands in what happened to me. But I had no prove, so I could not just accuse him of doing that.

We were all seated and the Eze greeted us. He announced what the gathering was all about. But before he continued, he demanded that the two parties involved should present their presents. These were the things we were told to bring last time we gathered. My uncle was the first to bring his. He even did more than we were ordered to do. Having inspected and approved our presents, the council then called on us to bring our evidences to the disputed portions of land. Without wasting time, my uncle jumped out with some papers, and handed them over to the council secretary, who was expected to read them to everyone's hearing. But before it could be read, I was called upon to bring my own evidences. I stood up to explain my encounter few hours back, but there was noise everywhere. It was started by my uncle and his supporters. Within few minutes, everywhere became quiet, and I was ordered to continue with my stories. I narrated how I was ambushed. My story was real, but it was taken for moonlight tales. There was another moment of confusion and noise making. This time around, the Eze calmed the council down. He asked me what I think the council could do from there. I was helpless and knew nothing more to say. I was convinced that my uncle had planned everything to deal with me. I later told the council to follow the case in the most justifiable way. My uncle was then called upon to make a comment. In his speech, he concluded that since I had no evidence to show the council, the truth of the matter was that I had no basis for my claims, and that meant that the lands were his own and therefore I should leave his land for him. A few council members were allowed to talk, but their contributions were all in line with my uncle's.

Conclusively, the Eze ruled that since I had no evidence, the custom requires that in a case like this, the complainant had to bring juju for the defendant to swear. It was a nice verdict any way, but my uncle refused the verdict. He insisted that we should be judged based on the evidences provided and if not; he would do anything possible to take over the land. Even if it would cost him his last drop of blood.

The judgment has been passed; everyone was waiting for the next line of action. When I got home that day, your mother and your grandmother were waiting worrisomely. By then, your mother was six months pregnant. When I broke the news that it has gotten to the stage of swearing an oath, your grandmother slumped and died. Being afraid and helpless about the whole situation, and considering your mother's condition, I decided to keep quiet over the whole issue. Although I knew that my quietness will have an adverse interpretation to my uncle. They would believe that I have decided to forget the parcels of land because within a short while, I lost my parents and your mother was not strong enough to back me up.At any case, I was ready to forget the land instead of being in enmity with my people or even hurting your pregnant mother.

After two weeks of my mother's burial, I had a trance. My dead father appeared to me crying. I tried to console him, but the more I tried, the more he kept crying. At a point, he started walking away from me. Immediately, my dead mother also appeared and scolded him (my father) for behaving the way he was doing. She told him that I am still their only son and should not be left alone. It was then that my father called me to get his matchet and follow him to the farm. That has been his routine when he was alive. He would always like me to accompany him to the farm. Immediately we walked out for the farm, he told me to hold strongly anything he had given me even when he was not around. He further told me that someone in his absence would come to forcefully take the things he left for me, but that I should be strong. As we moved further, he showed me our farmlands. These lands were being farmed by outsiders. My father instructed me to go and tell the people not to work there again. As I moved out to deliver his message, he disappeared.

That morning, I was lionized to fight for what belongs to me. I immediately walked down to one of my farmlands, and to my greatest bewilderment, the land had been cleared. Luckily for me as I was going back home, I saw my uncle in the company of some youths who were doing the work for him. I then realized that he was the one working on the farmland. Fearlessly, I warned him to discontinue working on that land in order for peace to reign. But he never took me seriously. Instead threatened that if I do not stay away from his path, I will join my weak father soon.

Calling my father weak was the greatest insult that unleashed the man in me. I furiously left without uttering any other word. For the rest of the day, what I was thinking was how I would start up a fight against my uncle while your mother was still about to put to bed.

As though she knew what I was thinking, your mother whispered to my troubled ear that she was ever ready to stand by me no matter what. Those words energized me greatly. The following day, I consulted our community headman telling him to gather the elders for me. During the meeting, I told them that I was ready to do anything in order to prove that I am the owner of the disputed parcels of land. My uncle objected by telling me to get ready to swear the Amadioha for him the next Afo market day. He thought that I would not accept to take the risk. Amadioha is a dreaded juju in Igboland. One dares not joke with the juju because it has no mercy. Although it is a just deity because once consulted in a case, it is obvious that the truth must be unveiled. But one deadly thing about it is that it never completes her assignment without taking lives of the erring party or striking them with ailments.

Although Amadioha has great powers and is a just oracle, people hide under his wings to pervert justice. A story was told of one Obiakpo who was a very wicked man in the neighboring village of Ndufu. Obiakpo had land dispute with his brother Chimdi who was the true owner of the embattled land. It was said that Obiakpo threatened to invite the almighty Amadioha to the case, which Chimdi accepted. After the oath was sworn Chimdi returned to his house relaxed. The Amadioha priest always warn disputing parties on the dangers of involving in any act of charms, within one year of administration of the oath. However one month after the oath, Chimdi lost his first son. On the burial day, his wife equally died. Before two months could pass, all of Chimdi's livestock were dead. At the seventh month of the oath, Chimdi got mad. The quick succession of these terrible happenings got the whole village bewildered. Even those that believed that the disputed land was Chimdi's were no longer certain of what they knew. Amadioha is not an unjust oracle, and cannot be influenced. How come Chimdi faced all these? Some queried. But the question remained unanswered. It was only Obiakpo and the then Amadioha Chief priest that could tell exactly what happened. Two of whom were not ready to expose themselves. Although the oath seemed to have justified Obiakpo as the true owner of the land, some elders in Ndufu community could not believe it. Even my uncle who was Obiakpo's friend once asked rhetorically, "could it be that Amadioha is not Amadioha again?" He asked himself this question when he heard the news of Chimdi's predicaments. This was because he believed that the land in question was not Obiakpo's. But how was this made possible? Only the gods could answer.

Although the shock of Chimdi's fate shook me, I strongly believed that my own case was exceptional. I am the true owner of the lands in question and again, Amadioha never kills an innocent man. Seeing that I have made up my mind to swear the oath, my uncle reminded me of the fate that befell Chimdi. He did this to put fear into me. I remembered my father's warning in my dreams not to let go what he kept for me. He also assured me of his protection and directive whenever the need arises. Barely two weeks before your mother put to bed, all roads led to Obiakpo's compound. His four wives and thirty-eight children were wailing as though they were thrown into the abyss of everlasting agony. No titled man was seen going to his compound. But any other person in both our village and Ndufu village were trooping in and out. I never knew what was happening till when your mother came back from the market that day. She told me that Obiakpo died the previous night after making some confessions. He confessed how he collaborated with the Chief Priest of Amadioha to use a different Ofo in order to deal with Chimdi. According to her, after the day Chimdi took the oath, Obiakpo started haunting his family. He used charms to cause all the evil that befell Chimdi in order to falsely claim that it was Amadioha that dealt with the family.

Finally, when the matter was streamlined that I would swear an oath, we were told of the things to bring for the D-Day and the meeting was dismissed. Throughout that week, I made myself sacred and would always come out in the middle of the day and night to plead my case. On 29th June, 1989 we all matched to Ihuala for the oath. My son, it was a scene you would not like to behold. I marched naked to Ihuala to swear the Amadioha.

I have to infer that the death of Obiakpo brought rest to your mother and I. I never knew before that day that my uncle had inquired from Obiakpo how he manipulated the almighty Amadioha to his favour. My uncle toed that same line to annihilate your mother and I so that he would seem to have been justified by Amadioha. It was from the day Obiakpo died that the nightmares and all the ordeals your mother and I were passing through were eliminated

Friday 29th June, 1990 made it exactly one year I swore the oath. On that day, my compound was filled with friends and well-wishers. Different types of dishes were prepared. Eze-Amadioha and all the titled men in Umuagba had done the commemoration ritual before noon. At about 3pm, the atmosphere was very dense. Everyone concluded that it would rain heavily that day. Within some seconds, there was a flash of lightening followed by a very heavy thunder storm. Immediately after that, there was a very mighty wind. It was so aggressive that nobody could dare to move an inch. Within few minutes, the weather was normalized. People were surprised by the dramatic display that evening. Shortly after this, there was wailing from my uncle's compound. The thunder did not only strike him dead, but the mighty wind carried the roof of his house to an unknown destination. It was indeed not a surprise to many. They knew that Amadioha had visited the defaulter. On that same day, my Uncle's corpse was disposed at the Oke-Acha stream.

But even at that, some of the villagers were not happy with our family because we survived what they thought was dead for us. And even till date, most families are not happy with us especially my uncle's family. But God has been so faithful to us. Your younger brother, Ogumka is now growing in strength and health. I guess it is the same transfer of hatred that you and your siblings are passing through"

## CHAPTER TWO

# THE CHILD

**OGUMKA WAS** fast growing; his name has been shortened to Mka. As a child, he used to think that life is all about eating, playing, sleeping, and crying when he needed attention. Little did he know that there were more and more things life could give. In those days, Obiageri was always in soup whenever Mka wanted something and failed to get it at that point. He would cry so carelessly that the mother would look for a way to settle him at once. She knew that shouting at him or even flogging him would worsen the situation. One of Mka's best times was during the weekend. Living in Umuahia since 1991, Odu had never seized to come home every weekend. When coming back, he would buy Mka lots of goodies. As the only child at home, Mka had no one to hustle it with. The way he ate made the parents nicknamed him Odighi nkem juru. Life was to Mka a bed of roses.

He was four years then. Within a short while, he discovered that the mother's belly had started protruding. He thought it was as a result of feeding well; to him, nothing else could cause one's belly to be that big if not food. One day, he asked his mother why her stomach was that big. She told him that a baby was inside. Baby? Mka inquired. Why is it inside your belly? Who put it there, you? Will you bring it out in the latrine? Instead of answering the questions, Obiageri started singing. Though Mka was stubborn, he had manners. He was taught through folktales that when one is singing, he is communicating with a supreme being and thus needs no distraction.

One Friday morning, Mka saw his mother shading tears. That was the first time he saw her crying. He was sorry for her, though he neither knew why she was crying, nor could help her. One of the things that baffled him most was that she was rolling up and down her bed as she cried. "Mummy ndo, mummy ndo" was his sympathetic utterance as he tried to cuddle her. At a point, she sent him to go and call Aunty Chinenye for her. Aunty Chinenye was a nurse. Although she studied neither nursing nor anything related to medicine, she knew her job very well. She was normally called Nurse Eliza owing to the fact that she was a nurse in western system, but without formal training. He ran to aunty Chinenye's house but unfortunately, she was not available. She was on day shift as he was later told. Mka went back and reported to the mother that Aunty Chinenye was not there. She told him to go and take his food and that she was going to the hospital because of stomach ache. On hearing that his mother was having stomach ache, Mka lost appetite; "How can I be eating when mum is crying to the hospital", he thought. She bade him good bye and left. Mka was hungry, he had nothing else to do; after all, he had shown her his sympathy and had gone to Aunty Chinenye's house. So he went in for his food.

Within a while, Aunty Chinenye visited, with a smile on her face. "Jikere ka anyi ga lee nne gi" she told Mka. Mka replied that his mother went to the hospital because she had stomach ache. "Amam na ogara ulo ogwu, mana osi mbia kpota gi". As soon as he heard that she sent her to come and bring him, he rushed into the room, wore his previous year's Christmas clothes and followed her. On their way to the hospital, Mka asked her how she was doing; he also asked her if the pains she was passing through had subsided. She told him that his mother was fine and had given birth. This sounded strange to him. He did not know what she meant by that; but he did not argue any more. As they reached the hospital, Mka saw his mother breast-feeding a baby. Her stomach had reduced to an extent. He was speechlessly happy. He gazed at her, but had refused to go closer to her even when she bade him to come. He wanted to be by her side, but was afraid of the thing sucking her breast. He thought the baby would bite him if he moved closer. When Obiageri discovered that her son was afraid of the baby, she told him it was his younger sister and that she had born her for him. As if the baby wanted Mka to get closer to their mother, she slept. It was when Obiageri laid her in the bed that Mka was able to go close to his mother. She carried him and pecked him, but that never called his attention. He was busy watching his sister with intense devotion. Obiageri asked him if he liked her but he did not reply.

Mka was ten years old when he observed that events were not unfolding on his family's favour. Last six years, his two senior brothers-Isinna and Ezeji were sent to Lagos to live with Aunty Rebecca while his father was then based in Umuahia. Obviously, he has been wondering why his peers would be dressed by their parents in a uniform every morning. The children in their uniforms would go in groups to Umuama in the morning and would return in the afternoon. Mka had over the time pondered on this. He knew nothing about this departure in the morning and returning in the afternoon. The only thing he could explain was that his peers wear clothes that looked alike and carry bags of different sizes during this journey. One day, during moonlight play, Mka asked his friend- Ugo where they always go in the day time. "We go to school" replied Ugo.

"What do you mean by that and what exactly do you do there?" Ugo told him that they always go to school to see their Madam who always tell them to recite ABC and 123. "Sometime, our madam will tell us the story of Jesus Christ who was hanged on a cross, some other times, she would tell us another thing".

The whole thing impressed Mka who made up his mind to go with them the following day to see the madam. It was on Wednesday morning; Ugo had gone to Odu's house to check on his friend, Mka who had said the previous night that he would follow him to school. That day, Mka tried to sneak out from her mother for school, but he could not succeed because Obiageri was a very careful woman. She would always read their movements even before they make them. Ugo left Mka's house that morning very disappointed in Obiageri who could not allow them to play their games the way they had planned. On his own side, Mka was very angry with his mother. He could not eat for the rest of the day because he was thinking of how he would have enjoy being with Madam in school and hear the story of Jesus Christ whom Ugo had earlier tipped him was hanging on the cross.

The following day, Mka tried the same prank, but this time around, Obiageri was not in any way friendly with him. She flogged him mercilessly that Thursday morning and warned Ugo not to come to take Mka to school until they get him registered. For the rest of the day, Mka cried as though everything depended on crying. He wondered why Obiageri could not allow him to go and hear the story of Jesus Christ. But in as much as his day was defined by weeping, he found solace whenever the voice of Obiageri re-echoed "till when he is registered". This gave him hope that he would soon be a school boy.

Although Odu heard of Mka's plot to sneak out for school the previous day, he never took it seriously. He thought it was a story cooked up by Obiageri to facilitate her children's enrolment in school. His thought in this line was because Obiageri had been giving him sleepless nights about the children's formal education. When the same story was repeated on Thursday night by Obiageri, he began to believe that something has to be done to send his son to school. He then summoned Mka and queried him on why he was trying to pull his mother's legs. Mka could not utter any word because he knew that his mother's beating would be a mere romance when compared with what Odu does to any of his children that errs. Although nothing much was discussed about that that night, Odu had finally concluded plans with Obiageri to enroll their wards to school. After all, the academic year just started on Monday that week.

It was a very happy day for Mka. He was ten years old then. On that day, Obiageri woke and bathed him as early as 6:00 am. She had earlier told him that he would be enrolled in primary school. After bathing him, Mka ran into the room, applied a local cream and wore his blue short with a red polo. He felt he was a big boy in his new polo, though the space between his contours and the cloth could still accommodate two more people of his size.

By 7:00am, they were on their way to the school. Mka was filled with zeal and enthusiasm, and was happily carrying his slate on his head while holding her with the other hand.

It took them not less than an hour to be at the school. The morning assembly was almost over when they got there. At that point, the headmistress was making announcements. Among all she said, one of the things that sink into Mka was, "this is Umuama Primary School Izoke, where foundations are laid for future leaders". After which, she taught the pupils one song in Igbo language. She also acknowledged that there were first timers in the school. She advised the old pupils to treat the new ones like their brothers and sisters.

Within few minutes, the assembly was over. As others were retiring to their classes, Mka stood in confusion. Obiageri had gone, he was left stranded. Where was he supposed to go? Which class did he know was for primary one pupils? After a while, the headmistress bade him to come, but fear could not allow him to step an inch. The next thing he heard was "Mka bia nga". He was surprised that she knew whom he was. Mka summoned courage and went to her. It was then she told him that his father had earlier told her about his coming to school that day. She took him to primary one class room.

In the class were about fifteen pupils who registered the previous week. Mrs. Udenze a tall, black woman from Umuagu was the most talked about Madam. She was a very kind woman who would always come to school with biscuits to share to her pupils. Little wonder Ugo never stopped telling Mka about the Madam. He has many good things about her. The gesture Madam showed them made them to forget that that day was their first day in school. They were very relaxed and easily associated with pupils who came from Umuagba. Another thing that Mka personally loved about Madam was the way she taught them. But it was quite unfortunate that Madam never told the story of the Jesus Christ who was hanging on a cross. One of the things that propelled Mka to school.

Mka started making new friends from the second day in school. As the days passed, he discovered that the bond between him and Ugo in school began to loosen. Each of them began to spend time with newly made friends. During break, they would storm the school farm in cliques, visiting all the palm trees in the farm in search of either palm fruits or kernels. They would after cracking the kernels put them into their water bottles. The biggest boy then was anyone who had the largest number of palm kernels in his water bottle. Their break time normally lasted for forty-five minutes, after which, they had one more class before dismissal.

Another period they enjoyed most was their way back home. The school dismissed by 1 pm, but they would spend not less than four hours on their way home. During that time, they would complete the plays they were unable to finish during break time. On reaching Mbara, (a track road with bushes on both sides), they would all enter the bush to ease themselves. Every one of them had to go, whether pressed or not. There in the bush, they would all squat irrespective of gender, pushing as if they were in labour. After that, they would clean their anus with leaves. One stupid thing they did on daily basis was to check whether the excreta they dropped the previous day was the way they left them.

This routine continued for the whole academic session. By the next session, some elements of maturity had taken place. Mka had entered primary two. Notwithstanding that he was the brightest pupil in his class, he could speak only Igbo. He was born in a village where everything was done in their native way and he had started schooling very late. Even in school, their teachers taught them in Igbo language. Although Mka could hear English language when spoken, but could not speak it fluently for thirty seconds.

One day, the school headmaster gathered all the teachers and class monitors of the whole school and announced that the federal ministry of education has set up an English exam for all primary two pupils before they could be qualified to cross over to primary three. He therefore warned all the class teachers to put in their best to make sure that the pupils learnt how to speak, read and write English language before they could get to primary three.

When they retired to their various classes, Mrs. Egu who was primary two teacher called out Mka and mandated him to be writing the names of noise makers and those that speak vernacular in the class. She gave him two different exercise books for the assignment. She further announced that anyone found guilty of speaking vernacular would pay the class the sum of Ten Naira as many times as the name appeared on the list, while noise makers would work in the school farm, during the break.

Mka has gotten a new responsibility in school. The new development had some effects on both the school and the pupils. One of which was that the classes were never as noisy as they used to be. Although the pupils would always have something to say, they could not express themselves in the legitimate language. The best they could do was to speak Engli-Igbo which only few could do. Another effect of the new development was that it made the class monitors to be seen as gods. In each class, the pupils all wanted to be in good terms with the class monitors in order not to have their names written in their black book. On the other hand, the stubborn boys in the classes would not want to comply with the new development and at the same time decided not to be subject to the class monitors. One day, Mka wrote down the name of Obiefule who was a notorious noise maker in the whole school. Obiefule was not only a noise maker but also a very strong and hefty boy. His physical prowess gave him the name-Agu. In spite of the fact that he was in primary two, nobody in the entire school could challenge him in wrestling, not to talk of fighting. This made him not to be afraid of the new development. During break, Obiefule was given a very large portion of grass to cut as his punishment. Those that went close to him as he was doing the punishment said that he had threatened to teach Mka the lesson of his life after school that day. When school dismissed, Obiefule went to Mbara and ambushed Mka. That day, he beat Mka till he was unconscious. None of the pupils had the courage to go close to them not to talk of separating them. Mka could not go to school the following day because he was seriously dealt with.

The following day, Mka resumed school. Trekking every morning from his village through Mbara to school has exposed Mka to the sight of many Umuehie women who always passed them on their way to their farms. One of such women was Mama Matina,who began to admire the boy. One day, Mama Matina approached Obiageri and indicated her interest to take Mka to live with her in Umuehie. After many discussions with Mka's parents they finally agreed to let Mka live with her.

Life for Mka was fun in Mama Matina's house. Although the young man always woke up very early to fetch water at Dimeke before going to school, things were indeed better for him than at home. After school, Mka usually go to Umuobike to help Mama Matina in the farm. Although he was very strong, and could work more than his madam expect from him; he never liked going to Umuobike. One of the things that made him to hate going there was that it involved passing through a very lonely and fearful bush track for about forty-five minutes. During this time, one had no other companion than birds and mosquitoes. Umuobike was the most fertile place within and, as a matter of fact, was always filled with farmers.

Even though Mka hated going to Umuobike to farm, he liked it for few things. One of the reasons why he liked Umuobike was the availability of wild animals there. It was when he started going there to farm that he first saw a live glasscutter, antelope, deer, and viper and so on. They were rampant in Umuobike bush.

One day, he was clearing the bush with his madam when he saw something with scales like a dried leave. He was surprised at that sight and called his madam's attention. "Ihea bu Ajuala" she said. As stupid as the snake could be, it never thought it wise to run for its life. Mama Matina struck it uncountable times with one big stick she had earlier cut. For the rest of the day, Mka did no further work. When they were about to leave, Mama

Matina took the snake and rapped it with palm frond. Mka was surprised and wondered what she wanted to do with the snake. When they reach the village square, they off-loaded their loads to have some relief. Mama Matina took the snake to one Mr. Ediahonu. This man was an herbalist. He also liked doing some strange things. It was later that Mka realized that his madam sold the snake to him. Mka hated serpents because of the deceitful act Bro Mathew told them the snake did to Eve and Adam her husband in the Garden of Eden.

One Saturday, precisely an Afo market day, Mka and Mama Matina were going to the farm to harvest cassava. On reaching to Ogboto-ukwu (a big gathering arena) Mka saw not less than fifty men with so many dogs. He had heard that hunters within Izoke, Umuagba, Umuchi, Umuohuru and Umueze had a hunting guild. He had also heard that they normally visit any member village for hunting during the village's market days. But he never thought they were up to the number he saw that day. They were so organized that they had a chairman, vice chairman, secretary, financial secretary, provost/PRO, and so on. They also had two uniforms. Then during hunting days, the host village would provide certain numbers of yam tubers with necessary ingredients for cooking them. The meal would be prepared with part of the games they caught. Another interesting thing about this people was that before they move out for the day's work, they normally partitioned themselves into groups. There were those that shoot, those that carry already killed animals, those that act as monitors and those that sing heroic songs that motivate their hunting dogs. These dogs were also adorned with the Ikpo. The Ikpo does three things in hunting expedition. One of which was to keep motivating and energizing the dogs. It was said that any dog that wears Ikpo never gets tired because the sound of the Ikpo gives it strength. Another function of the Ikpo was to frighten wild animals. With the ringing Ikpo, any animal that hides in a particular place would be aware of the emergence of an enemy. And upon so hearing, they rally around in search of refuge. This exposes them to hunters who would shoot them. Then the final function of the Ikpo was to distinguish between an approaching wild animal and a hunting dog. That is to say, hunter would only shoot anything seen or unseen, provided the thing was not ringing bell.

Chu ya! Chu ya! Chu ya! Tagbuo! Tagbuo! Tagbuo! Was a sound that Mka was hearing in their farm as they were harvesting cassava. In the first instance, he could only hear the sound, but could not decipher any word from the sound. The sound kept coming closer and closer. At a point, he started hearing the sound of Oja. Though the sound was thrilling, he was not at ease. Having remembered that they saw Ndi-nta when they were coming, he knew they were the people making the approaching sound. Mka waited for Mama Matina to react to what was happening, but she did nothing. At a point, he heard a very thunderous sound. It was so great that he could no longer restrain himself. It was the sound of a gunshot. He asked Mama Matina if she could hear anything. "Yes", she replied. He suggested that they should leave before the hunters could get to where they were. Instead of granting his request, Mama Matina told him that the hunters knew that people were around. She further asked him if he heard sound of Oja. He nodded in affirmative. She told him that that signified that the hunters had earlier seen them. It surprised him to hear that. Mama Matina could see despair in his face. She sat him down under one Ugba tree and explained to him certain things about hunting. Among the things she told him which he did not know before then was that hunters hunt with charms.

She said, "There was a traditionally prepared medicine called Uji-imi Nkita. It was traditionally believed that dogs have some mystical powers in their nostrils. It was the power that enables dogs to trace anything they can perceive. So in order to utilize this power, traditionalists have devised a way of using the nostrils of dogs mixed with some herbs to find any missing thing or to trace anything the hunters also use it in hunting expeditions. They use theirs in detecting if people are farming around the areas they are hunting. If they so discover, there will be random sounds of Opi and Oja to alert the shooters that people are around".

That was a very interesting but impromptu lecture

from Mama Matina. But Mka's attention towards what she was telling him was disrupted when an antelope, as big as a matured sheep ran across where they were. He became frightened though delighted by the sight of the animal. Within few seconds, it was as if all the wild animals in the bush were on a race. Gun shots were going up and down. At a point he heard something barking as it was running. It was a very big Ediabali. In the first instance, Mka thought it was one of the hunting dogs; he never knew Ediabali could bark until that day.

Within a while, everywhere was pacified. The hunters had gone to another hunting ground, Ihuala.

They finished work on time that day but, Mama Matina was not in a hurry to go. When they got to Ogboto-ukwu, everywhere was full of dead animals. Mka knew that bush meat was always cheaper during hunting days, but he did not know that hunters could have as big catches as he saw that day. Buyers came from nearby villages and markets to buy meat for both commercial purposes and personal consumption.

Without minding that people were waiting to buy meat, the hunters all sat down to eat their yam. The yam has been cooked before they came out from the bush. According to their custom, the first two animals killed would be sent home instantly for preparation by any woman they may choose. This was to make sure that the food was ready before the expedition was over. Mka watched them as they eat the delicious yam. It was that day that he realized that hunters eat bush meat more than people could imagine. The first two catches of that day were two big antelopes. So one would not be surprised at the chunk of meat each of them got

After their meal, the provost kept aside some of the big animals. Those ones were not to be sold. They are to be shared according to ratio, and some would also be thrown to the dogs. The left overs were then ripe for selling. People then approached and started indicating interest in any one they wished. It was only the provost with the help of the PRO that sold all the ones that were for sale. In order to be able to pay, Mama Matina and mama Udoka contributed money and bought one grasscutter. When they left, the hunters then shared the ones that had earlier been removed by their provost. It was a very interesting day for Mka. He made up his mind to be following Mama Matina to farm, especially during hunting days.

Within two months of Mka's stay with Mama Matina, he had become one of the most active Sunday School children of St. Peters Anglican Church. He was very interested in the church activities because Aunt Agatha and Sir Jonah would always tell them the stories of Jesus Christ and how Mother Mary usually gave him some fishes whenever she was making soup because Jesus was a good boy. Mka decided to imbibe the lifestyle of Jesus. He attended every church activity.

One Sunday evening during Sunday School session,

Bro. Mathew gave a teaching that changed Mka's life decision. That evening, Bro Mathew who was the Church Teacher at the Cathedral Church of St Peter gathered the children and told them the story of Joseph. He narrated how Joseph has been a good child from childhood. As such, his father made him a special robe and loved him so dearly. Joseph, according to him, was a virgin, and that made God to love him too. One day, Joseph was sold to one rich Mr. Potiphar whose wife was promiscuous. Mrs. Potiphar wanted to have carnal knowledge of Joseph, but the lad could not give in. This made the woman to cause misfortune for Joseph before Potiphar. But even in the face of these challenges, Joseph never gave up his virginity. As a matter of fact, God promoted him to be the second in command in Egypt.

After narrating this story, Bro Mathew led the children through a long session of sober reflection and prayers. Mka learnt that one has to cry bitterly for God to hear his prayers. That evening, he cried so profusely and prayed fervently too. He finally made a decision as Bro. Mathew instructed them. That day, Mka had a covenant with God, telling him that he would keep his virginity like Joseph. He beseeched God to bless and elevate him the same way he did to Joseph. The memory of that day made Mka to become a staunch follower of Jesus.

On July 27th, 2001, the Parish was observing her CMS anniversary at Anglican Church Umuama. That day, Mka recited the book of Psalms 121 off hand. His father was so impressed that he affirmed to his decision that his son would be a priest. After the event that evening, he took Mka to Bro Mathew and told him that he wanted to do what Elkenah and Hannah did to Samuel. He handed over Mka to Bro Mathew to bring him up in the ways of the Lord. That single event brought the end of Mka's life in Mama Matina's house. But the challenge was that Bro Mathew had no house then. He was squatting with a friend as there was no house in the Cathedral for him. He directed that Mka be taken to his friend Bro. Godwin's house. Seeing that Bro Mathew was not well settled to have Mka to be with him, Mka's parents decided that the lad live with them temporarily before he goes to Bro. Godwin's house.

At home, Mka who was then fifteen-years old became his father's friend. Having taken his Common Entrance exam from Primary five because of his intelligence. Mka had to stay at home for some weeks before his First School Leaving Certificate Exam. Because of how helpful he has proven to be, his father liked doing everything with him.

One evening, Mka's father requested him to accompany him to Onu-Acha stream to fetch water. It was around 7:30pm. Mka was holding his torch-light for him because he was carrying a wheel barrow. As they were coming back, Mka was surprised by what he saw. Being intoxicated by how bright the torch-light flashed, he was pointing it aimlessly. Sometimes, he would point it towards the sky, at other times, to his eyes. Odu never bothered about what he was doing with the torch-light because the moon was giving out its best that night. When Mka pointed the torch-light towards the Ikoro house, he saw two people posing like wrestlers. They held themselves very tight. The sight really surprised him. He was thinking of what could prompt those fellows to leave their house to a lonely Ikoro house that night to fight. Besides, that place was bushy and hidden. May be, they wanted to fight it over without anyone separating them, he thought. When he could no longer keep it to himself, he called his dad's attention. "Daddy lee ndi lugha ogu", he reported. As if they never wanted his father to see them, they immediately ran away. Odu told his son to leave them, "ihe ojoo gba afo, ya ghoo omenala…umuaka Ugbua na ihe ojoo…" he added. But Mka could not understand what he meant by that, and he gave no further concern to that because it was not his business.

After dinner that night, Mka left for a moon light play with his siblings. The glory of the moon light could even be seen by a blind man. It was as if God ordered the moon and all the stars in the sky to beatify that night. At the playground, the children had finished Kpukpukpu-gele play. It was time for folklores, and they all ran to Iguegbe's house. Iguegbe was the oldest man in Umuagba village. He was in his early 90s, but one may take him for a man in his 60s because of how strong he was. He was a successful hunter and a famous gunpowder baker in the whole community. His prowess in baking of gunpowder fetched him the name-Iguegbe. Stories had it that his wife died ten years after their marriage as a result of a mistake he made one hunting night.

That night, he forgot to place a mark of Nzu on his wife's fore face. It was said that night hunters, especially those who hunt in Ikpanta forest, normally do such before embarking on their hunting activity. The secret was that some evil spirits that live in that bush always took the form of wild animals at night. And being provoked by how hunters were killing them frequently, resorted to revenge. Thus, an evil spirit would invoke the soul of a hunter's loved one and appeared to the hunter in the form of wild animals. If the hunter kills the animal-spirit, it would take not more than a week, he would lose someone. One adage says "since birds learnt to fly without perching, hunters have started shooting without missing". When hunters started losing their relatives steadily, they consulted a Dibia who discovered the cause of the perils. The Dibia told them to always use Nzu on their relatives before they could go out in the night for hunting. Thus during the game, if any one sees an animal with white bleach, the person would know it was his relative and would not shoot.

But that night, Iguegbe forgot to do this because his wife had gone to bed earlier. He had never reach Ikpanta when he saw a very big Ediabali with no mark on its fur.

He quickly opened fire and the animal gave up. Within two days of that incident, his wife died with no child for him. Because of the love he had for the wife and to avoid killing another loved one, he decided not to marry again. Although he had no child, Iguegbe was a lover of children and the children loved him too. That was why they always go to his house to hear akuko-ifo during the moonlight.

> Iguegbe: Ifo cha kpii!
> Children: wooo
> Iguegbe: Nkita nyara akpa?
> Children: nshi ako n'ohia
> Iguegbe: osisi dachie uzo?
> Children: Nwanyi aria ya elu
> Iguegbe: okuko nyuo ahu?
> Children: Ala achuwa ya oso.

These lines always began their stay with Iguegbe before the main story of each night. That night, Iguegbe told them only one story. It was unlike him; but they could not question him. When he dismissed the children they retired to play Oro-oro. As usual, whenever they come out for moonlight play, they normally see youths in pairs at some hidden places. Though the children hear the sounds of their voices, none could say what they were discussing because it was usually with very low voices. Most times, voices of ladies sounding like those passing through pleasurable pains would be heard. One thing that baffled Mka most was that each pair was made up of a man and a woman, and they always held each other tight. To the poor Mka, that was fighting; because fighting was the only thing he knew that could make two people to be so close to each other and with hands across each other's body. But then, his puzzle was – what could always make people to come out at night not for a moonlight play, but for a fight?

When he got home that night, he asked his father why people would always like to fight in the night and in hidden places. His father asked him what he meant. Mka reminded him of the one that happened when they were coming from the stream few hours back. He told him that people do the same thing whenever they go out for moonlight play. Instead of giving Mka the direct answer that the boy needed, he told him that fighting is ungodly and that he should not befriend those fighters. He urged Mka to go to bed because it was late. As he was going to bed, Obiageri asked the husband whom the people they saw fighting were. She was told that it was not fighting but that they were having sex. "Odikwa egwu oo! Exclaimed Obigeri. When would incest stop in this community? She asked rhetorically.

They did not know that Mka was hearing what they were saying. It was that night that he learnt that sexual intercourse could be carried out while standing up. That night was his first time of seeing people having sex. So he thought about the scene for a while before he dozed off. From that night, he developed a deep sense of hatred for those he has seen in that act. Pre-marital sex was against moral lessons as Bro Mathew taught in the church.

Three weeks have passed since Mka returned from Mama Matina's house. He has shown how resilience and hardworking he was. This made the villagers to become jealous of Obiageri. They also used Mka as an example for their own children, especially those of them that were too lazy to go to school, or to learn any handiwork. All they were good at was to steal people's fowl, goats, sheep, and so on when they go out for their various businesses. They would kill and eat some of these animals while the rest were sold. In the evening, they roam from Ukwu-Ngwo to Obom aimlessly. Then around 7:30 pm, they would appear in pairs of boys and girls. Most of them even stayed on the tombs that were around the old church compound to have sex. The priests at St. Peter's Cathedral had announced, warned and lamented on the nemesis that awaited these immoral youths. But the more they warned, the more the atrocities.

In Umuagba then, a girl in her eighteen that has never committed abortion for up to three times was considered a virgin. Incest and other sexual immoralities were the order of the day. Abortion was rampant because if the child was allowed to be born, it would be unheard of that both parents were not only from the same village, but the same kindred or even family in some cases.

Parents were aware of these things, but they seem to promote them. A man could lie in his matrimonial bed with another man's wife or even daughter. A man and son could also lie under the same roof with women that were not their partners. Even most of the white clothed men in the Cathedral and other churches were part of this sacrilege. Because no one even the so called men of God in the community could throw the first stone if Christ should order that, the youths as such, were hardened in their lifestyles. Reports of Rev. Fr. Israel Amadi who was said to have had the taste of more than fifty percent of his female congregants was told. Fr. Israel was said to be a flaming priest serving at St. Mary's Parish. During his early days in the Parish, Fr. Israel would always organize revival programs that attracted thousands of people both within and without the Roman Catholic Church. Even the adoration has taken a new dimension as people fall, twerk, whirl and scream under the anointing; an occurrence that was not happening in the church previously. Although the people of Umuobike from where the Fr. was posted to St. Mary's spread the rumours of the Father's immoral lifestyle, the "miracles" he performed could not allow people to believe them. One night during Easter revival program he organized, it was reported that the Reverend Father had invited another man of God from another parish in order to give the church a variety. The invited man of God was said to have ministered throughout the night, but when the closing prayers were to be said, Fr. Israel whom it was his responsibility to do so was not in the church. The parish youth leader: Obinna had to go to the parsonage to call the Rev. Father. Unfortunately to the Father, the youth leader whose familiarity with him made him always to enter his bedroom with ease thought that the father was sleeping. When he got in that night, he caught the Rev. and Mrs. Agnes on bed having sex. He immediately rushed out and with the help of the invited Man of God; he dismissed the congregation without the resident priest coming out for the program that night. The following day, Fr. Israel invited the youth leader. When he came, he gave him some money and made him swear the Holy Bible not to tell anyone what he saw. He further told him that Mrs. Agnes was a barren woman; and that God revealed to him that the woman could not get pregnant because both the woman and the husband led very amorous lifestyle during their youthful days. He further said God revealed to him that the yoke denying the woman the gift of pregnancy could only be broken with seven days holy sex with a priest. That was what led him to the act, he explained. Sequel to the oath he swore, Obinna could not tell anyone what he saw. Instead, from that day, the two men became closer than they used to be. Obinna would always go to the parsonage, and each time he did, he would see the Fr. with a different woman both married and single ladies.

After Sunday Mass one evening, Obinna went to

see the Rev. Fr., and to his greatest surprise, he saw him taking cocaine with Rev. Sis. Salome and Agatha. The two Reverend Sisters had visited from Canada where they were on sabbatical. They invited Obinna to join them but he refused. Fr. Israel reminded him of the oath they had of which one of its terms was that they would do anything to please each other, no matter what it could be. Upon hearing how God could punish him if he hesitates, Obinna gave in. From that moment, he lost knowledge of where he was till the following morning. He woke up naked and in pains. He was experiencing an unexplainable pain in his anus. Later, he thought he was drugged and raped. But the pain was in his anus not genital organ. Besides, there were two women in the house, the Rev. Fr. whom he thought was not a gay had to enjoy the night with the ladies. He repulsed the thought of being rapped. When the Rev. Father discovered that he was awake, he bade him to go and have his bath as his breakfast was ready. Obinna was going to take his bath when he saw the two sisters fondly their various breasts so romantically in the sitting room. The ecstasy they were into was such that they could not even consider that someone was with them in the house. Even the Rev. Fr. was with them in the same room watching television after telling Obinna to go and have his bath. Obinna could not believe that the two women of God were lesbians. He then began to consider that Fr. Israel may have raped him when the ladies were busy on themselves last night. When he got to the bathroom, he saw the confirmation of his thought as the Fr. joined him in the bathroom and was telling him how beautiful his body was. Obinna who was both confused and ashamed as he was standing naked before the Rev. could not say anything. Before he could know what was happening, the Rev has put off his trousers and asked Obinna to permit him to join him in the bathroom. It was indeed a bad experience for Obinna that day, but he was bound by oath not to talk. Besides, the more his activities with the Rev. Fr, the more his wallet swells up. This made him to bear everything and face his miserable lifestyle. This lifestyle continued unwelcomely for Obinna till when Fr. Israel went on sabbatical to Italy. It was then that Obinna who was living another man's life all this while was able to expose some of the evils of Fr. Israel. Having heard of these stories, the youths could not fear anybody as they continued in their immoral lifestyle. Even Mka, was facing the challenges of living up to his decision in an immoral community.

The community was known as Sodom and Gomorrah of the 20th century then. With all these exposures, Mka has started having some feelings. He has been harboring some feelings for Linda, a very beautiful fair girl from Umuagu who had stayed in the neighborhood since her childhood. She was a year younger than Mka. Mka never felt for a girl the way he was feeling for Linda. He could not complete a whole day without trying to set his eyes on her. Although he was controlling his body reactions and feelings whenever he saw her, he knew she was crushing on him.

One day Mka was coming from Ukwu-ngwo when he saw her running in the opposite direction. He guessed she was not wearing bra that evening as her breasts were heaving left and right. The sight of this threw Mka to the Eden of sexual euphoria. His vein got helplessly erected as though it would sprout out from his trousers. He was tempted to hug her so that that dangling gland could at least quench his urge, but he was able to restrain himself. Mka could not eat that night; all he wanted was to give up his flower to Linda. Her thought never left him till he finally dozed off. It was not up to five minutes he slept when his vein became as stiff as a rod. Mka was with the girl he wanted to see in his dream. Linda was the one that approached the coy Mka and started making advances to him in that dream. Before he could know what was going on, they had started having a rough ride. A few minutes later, she was gone, as Mka was making effort to bring her back when he woke up. He immediately ran out from the room and cleaned up because his trouser was soaked with sperm as though he was poured two liters of water.

One day, Mka was tempted to be the man his fellow boys were. It was in the month of April. It had rained the previous day as if Noah was about to sail another ark. The day that followed witnessed sunshine. So it was obvious that they would go Mmum Mbele that night. By 8pm, they had their dinner and went out to meet other children at Okporama so as to move out in a group. Mka told his siblings to wait for him while he went to Linda's house. They thought he was going to call her for snail hunting, but he had an additional intention.

Immediately she saw Mka, Linda was very happy such that it was as though they had planned to meet that night. Before long, everyone was ready and they moved out for the snail hunting. The first place they went to was Umuokiri. There used to be a borrow pit there, but it was later filled up with refuse. Thus, snails were always in their numbers there. As soon as they entered into the bush, everyone went his way to gather as much snails as possible. Within five minutes everyone was already busy seeking and picking Mbele. Along the process, Mka met Linda in a lonely place. Linda was carrying her snail basket very close to her chest. Mka requested that she should show him her catch. She bent down a bit for Mka to see. As if he wanted to touch the basket, Mka tactically stroked her breast. He expected repulsion, but she did not utter any word. Rather she was helplessly gazing at Mka who was equally confused and knew nothing else to do at that point. They stood motionlessly for some seconds. She then dropped her basket and playfully whispered that she would stroke him back. "I have no breast, where are you going to stroke me?" asked Mka. Instead of an answer, her hand just went straight to

Mka's sex-starved vein that was as stiffened as a rod. That act just boosted Mka's morale. He fondled her breasts so gently that she immediately held him tight. But by then, Mka had no more interest in enjoying the sexual ecstasy that he longed for. He remembered the biblical Joseph; how Mrs. Potiphar was ready to give him sex and how Joseph resisted. They held each other for about two minutes with neither words nor further action. Obi, one of the boys in the snail hunting affair might have imagined why two Mpanaka had been in a particular place for some minutes and with no movement around it. When light started approaching the direction of Mka and Linda, they immediately disengaged themselves and parted ways. That night, Mka caught the least Mbele among all who went with them. Though he felt that he has messed himself up before Linda by not proving that he was a potent man, he was thankful to God for not falling into the sexual temptation.

## CHAPTER THREE

# THE CHURCH BOY

**BRO. MATHEW** has finally made arrangement for Mka to pack in with his friend: Bro Godwin. He was the resident pastor at St Peter's Extension Church. Bro Godwin is a tall handsome born again Christian. As a bachelor, he lived alone, though his sisters do visit him in alternation. They wanted to be sure that the pastor fed well because he is the fasting type of a Christian. At the extension church, Bro Godwin led many people to Christ. He did revival programs twice in a week. The way he prayed made the villagers believed that no matter how strong the devil may be, crossing Bro. Godwin's environment was a to suicide mission. Arranging for Mka to live with him was a very perfect arrangement because Mka's parents had wanted their son to be a staunch Christian. More so, considering that most church workers who have lived around were known for one social vice or the other, Bro Godwin who was the Saint of all was the right man for the soon to become man of God: Mka.

It was on Tuesday evening that Mka was taken to Bro Godwin's house. The poor Bachelor has prepared a pot of jollof rice. He received his young disciple so warmly with the meal. At about 9:00pm, he called Mka out for prayers before they could go to bed. The prayer session unlike what Mka has gotten used to was a very lengthy one. Night prayers in Mka's house never took more than ten minutes. The man of God at a point started speaking in another tongue. Before he could know what was going on, Mka has started snoring deeply. But he continued alone in his prayers. By 11 PM, the prayer was over. He woke Mka and informed him that the following day was a covenant day. It was Wednesday Prayer Band. As such, everyone was expected to fast all through the day till around 3pm. This news was not welcomed by Mka who was waiting for the day to break for him to have another plate of the delicious jollof rice. But what could he do? The pastor has spoken already.

By 4am on Wednesday, Bro Godwin was already up for Morning Cry. He would go from there to morning devotion in the church. It surprised him when he came back at around 6:30am and saw that Mka had swept everywhere and washed the plates. If there was no other thing he learnt in Mama Matina's house, Mka learnt to wake up very early to do his home chores. At about

8am, Bro Godwin instructed Mka to take his bath and dress up for prayers. At exactly 9am, everyone was in the church. It was time for the mid-week service. The prayer warriors, the singers, everyone was all there for the business of the day. That day, Bro Godwin preached from the book of Esther. He narrated the whole story of Esther and how she got favour for both herself and her kinsmen because she preserved herself for her God. This story seemed to be prepared for Mka alone. He liked hearing stories of biblical youths who challenged God with what they had and got blessing from God in return. During prayer session, Bro Godwin asked everyone to promise God something very special, Mka thus assured his God that he was going to remain a virgin till his wedding night. He also asked God for a favour as he has done to both Joseph and Esther whom their stories were told in the bible.

At a point during the prayers, a very shocking scream was heard. Within a moment, the whole church was silent as if everyone wanted the lady that screamed to say the prayers for everyone. Within a while, Bro Godwin said "Master speak for your servant is attentive". Mka was very confused by the whole incident. Who was the master? Where was he and what would he say and to who? Within a while, the lady that has previously screamed started saying "My servant, I have heard your cries, I have decided to use you to liberate this land. I have decided to use you to save souls. I have decided to use you to raise generations for myself. I have decided to use you to do great things. Cry no more for I am with you till the end of the age. As long as you remain faithful to me, I will lift you higher. Finally, my son, I want you to arrange for a Forty Nights of power-packed prayer session. I want to do great things in this church. This forty nights' program has to start from this night. At the end of the prayers, you would know that I am your God indeed. Be strong my son, be strong for I am coming very soon"

As soon as the lady finished saying this, Bro Godwin led the whole congregation into worship songs as though he has received a ticket to heaven. But Mka was very confused at the whole thing. He was wondering how a young girl would be addressing Bro Godwin as her son. The whole prophecy was imaginary to him. But there was nothing he could do about it, after all, the message was not for him. Before the prayer ended that day, Bro Godwin announced that there would be forty nights of prayers in the church that would kick-off that night.

Life in Bro Godwin's house has started for Mka. He was meant to sleep with prayers, dream of prayers and wake with prayers. He liked the environment because everyone loved him. He was seen as the pastor's son. That was a very big privilege for him. Mka does little work in the parsonage. Youth members, choristers, mothers and fathers' fellowships were always available to do the work for the pastor. But there was one work that the pastor always wanted Mka to do for himself: reading and studying the bible and praying at least thrice a day. He wanted Mka to be very close to God because that has been what his parents and Bro Mathew wanted of the poor boy.

One night, during the forty nights' program, Mka fasted like every other person during the day time. That day, he was more serious than the previous days. He wanted to witness God specially that night. So he has prepared for the adventure. The prayer had started and it was around 11:30pm. The pastor had ministered and made an Altar Call. Many people including Mka came out. He ordered everyone to raise their hands and confess their sins to God. People were doing that and were shading tears because of their sins. Mka was not left out. He was crying aloud as though he was the one that has nailed Master Jesus on the cross of Calvary. He confessed his sins and even claimed to have committed sins he never did in order for God to have mercy on him. At a point, the pastor told everyone to stop praying but remain silent. He started speaking in tongues. A short while into this, people began to shout on top of their voices. While others were screaming "fire, fire, please lord, reduce the fire, I would not do that again, I am sorry for my sins", others were saying different things. As for Mka, the whole prayer session has been messed up. He could no longer concentrate again. Discovering that he could not help himself, he went and sat down and started watching the pastor and the prayer warriors casting and binding the congregants. For more than one hour, the whole place was agog. One of the persons being prayed for was Linda. It was alleged that she married several husbands in the marine world. During the prayer session that night, she was the first to start spinning. Before long, she fell on the church desk and broke her head. It was bleeding but no one cared about that. Everyone believed that the evil spirit in her would not allow her to feel the pain. As if that was true, Linda never relented from spinning aimlessly and screaming. At a point, the pastor held her, touched her breast and started binding the marine spirit which he claimed was on her two breasts. When it was known that Linda's case could not be settled that night, the pastor ordered the prayer warriors to take her into the church vestry and lock her up there. No one even cared about the blood that has painted everywhere. That night was indeed a mysterious one for Mka. He never knew prayers could be done the way it was done that night.

It was the fortieth night since the program started. Bro. Godwin told everyone the previous night to be well prepared for the bottom pot blessing on the final day. As such, the whole church was filled with people even some hours before 9pm when the event supposed to kick-off. The topic of that night was "GOD OF THE ELEVENTH HOUR, BREAK MY YOKE" In his preaching, Bro Godwin explained that God works in a mysterious way and that there were people whose prayers were waiting for the last night to be heard. He assured everyone that the night was going to be extraordinary. After the preaching, it was time for prayers. He called out all the children and youths to the podium for special prayers. As that was going on, people were falling on what was believed to be under the anointing. Linda was the first as usual. That night was not a friendly one for her and her marine spirit. As soon as she fell, the pastor shared his prayer squad. A group was to continue prayers with other congregants present while the pastor and some other invited men of God were to sort it out that night with Linda and her spirit team. Bro Joshua was said to be an evangelist who has visited from Aba. Because of his spiritual doggedness, he was nicknamed the Oracle. Bro Joshua before praying for Linda first of all, explained that the name Linda has a connection with the goddess of snake. And as such, Linda was possessed by the snake spirit. Other spirits that were said to be in Linda were the spirit of dog. The Oracle explained that Linda's amorous lifestyle was the handiwork of the dog spirit which according to him, was a chronic sex machinery spirit. After all these expositions and analysis of the spirits possessing Linda, he quoted many scriptural passages that gave him authority over those spirits. He also challenged the spirits to leave Linda whom he claimed was one of the daughters of Abraham. After some very long scriptural quotations, he bid Linda to come. Like an insane person. Linda walked lackadaisically to him, making gestures as though she wanted to seduce the Oracle. At that point, prayer rain kicked-off on Linda. As usual, she started screaming profusely. But that night's was a different one. Instead of screaming "fire! Fire" like before, she was instead screaming that she needed some time for herself. The Oracle told her that her time has expired. Before long, Linda started rolling on the floor, with her skirts rolled up to expose her whole private parts. She was not wearing pants. It was a free show for those who did not close their eyes. Her blouse was not left behind as it rolled up to unveil her succulent and very fresh breasts. Immediately, the oracle called upon one of the sisters around to get scarf to cover her. That did not go down well with some boys who were enjoying the free sight. Mka's innocent vein has already started kicking his trousers.

To the oracle, exposing Linda's cubicles was a ploy by the evil spirit to divert his attention. He was so determined not give in to the distraction. For over thirty minutes, the prayer clinic was hot on Linda. At a point, she screamed with a very loud voice "I want to confess, I want to confess. The fire is much on me. Please let me confess so that you will let me go, please, please, please I am ready to confess now". At this point, everywhere was quiet. The prayers ceased for the confession to be made. "I did not enter into her freely; I was invoked by her mother. She invited me into her when she was pregnant.

I met her in her dreams one night. I appeared to her like a beautiful young lady on her way to the stream. She begged me to help her fetch a bucket of water which I did. She said having helped her, my reward would be that her daughter would be like me both in physique and character. Since that day, I saw her as my friend. When she finally gave birth to Linda, I then decided to endow her with both my beauty and character. I have been protecting and giving her everything she wanted in life. I have never stopped giving her any man she had wanted even though she is still a girl of fourteen years. She has slept with more than eighteen different men. I have protected her in such a way that no man could neither impregnate nor infest her. The only man she has wanted so dearly to taste his vein but failed was Mka. The day I arranged for them Mka was not responding well before someone intervened. But even at that, I have vowed to give her the boy her mind has so desired either now or later because she has exchanged fluid with him in their individual dreams. Please let me go, you can have her. But note that I have not hurt her for once. I have been a good guider and a friend of hers" The whole church was plunged into silence which was broken by a worship song raised by the oracle. After some minutes of the song, Linda stood up from where she was lying and went straight for her seat.

The confession did not go down well with Mka. He was invited by the Oracle for deliverance. He was asked to kneel down with his hands raised up. Prayers of deliverance were rained on him. Unlike Mka who would always remain unmoved during deliverance sessions, he started staggering. Before long, he fell under the anointing for the first time. The prayer team liberated him from any covenant he has unknowingly entered with Linda. After some minutes of prayers, the oracle announced that Mka was a special instrument for God. That was the reason God has always made out ways for him no matter what the devil plan.

Finally, the Oracle called out Bro Godwin to the podium. He instructed that everyone should stretch forth their hands towards him for prayers. He announced that the Holy Spirit has revealed to him that Bro Godwin would be favored by the Lord Bishop of the diocese. That night was indeed epochal as Bro Godwin earlier announced. The prayer ended at about 4:30am.

By the following week, Bro Godwin received a letter of his admission into the theological college Umuahia. That meant that Mka would have to go home to stay with his parents until school resumes.

It was more than four years. Mka seemed to have lost contact with Bro Godwin since the later left for the theological college. One day, Mka got a letter from his home church after Sunday worship. When he opened the letter, it was Bro Godwin writing to him from the theological college. He requested Mka to inform him in writing how life has been right from the day he left for the theological college till date. He also attached to the envelope a copy of Igbo Bible and Ekpere na Abu because he heard that Mka was then a youth leader in his home church and a staunch chorister. Mka's letter took him two days to be ready. The letter reads thus:

## MY EXPERIENCE IN MOUNT HOREB SEMINARY

Dad had never called me for a discussion before that day. This was a night after my return from your house. The first thing he told me was to feel free to talk to him. This he said because he discovered that I was nervous. I thought that he had called me to ask me what I did with Linda during the snail hunting night as the prophecy revealed in the church. But my mind started relaxing when he said he was proud to have me as a son. He brought out a booklet he was holding. It was my report card; from primary one through primary five. My worst result as contained in the card was in primary four, second term. In that term, I was sick during the exam, and could not write Social Studies and Elementary science exams. When the result came out, I took third position in the class.

Having flipped through the report card, dad told me that I made him proud with my primary education, and as a matter of fact, he would like me to be in one of the most prestigious secondary schools within our locality. As if he has never made up his mind already, he asked me to make a choice of a secondary school I would like to attend. Without wasting time, I told him that I would like to study in Mount Horeb Seminary School Umuala. As a child, I did not choose the school because of what it was. Rather, I was fascinated by what I have seen its students enjoying. For instance, I knew of my cousin- Ikechi Barth who was a student of the school. Anytime he is going back to school, his parents would buy him Chocolate, Milk, Cornflakes, sugar, Juice and lots more. As if that was not enough, they would give him not less than 500 Naira for his pocket. Then, on monthly interval, he must be visited with another set of goodies. More so, whenever Ikechi came home, he became the center of our attraction. Everyone wanted to be his friend, and this made him to be seen as Oyibo among us. All these things enjoyed by Ikechi were what made me to tell dad that I would like to study in Mount Horeb.

Dad paused for a while. He broke the silence by asking me why I had chosen Mount Horeb. I told him that I would like to be a Bishop when I grow up, and studying in Mount Horeb would prepare me. He smiled and paused again. This time, he broke the silence by telling me that he has heard what l said. He told me to go and get him water to drink. After drinking the water, he told me that I would be going to Mount Horeb with him the following Saturday for a common entrance exam.

ANYANWU TIMOTHY CHIBUIKE

He further advised me to study hard so as to be admitted on merit. I nodded affirmatively.

As I was walking away, I felt I was on top of the world. I started envisaging how I would be enjoying my beverages. Although we often take tea at home, it was under mum's supervision. But this time around, I would be the master of myself. As I was leaving, I looked back. I saw dad smiling at me as if I was his lover. That inspired me more. Within me, I concluded he was smiling because he was proud of me. Of course, he must be. I walked straight to where I used to drop my school bag. That enthusiasm of being a boarding student of Mount Horeb was burning high in me. I wanted to start carrying out dad's instruction and advice: to study hard so as to be admitted on merit- with immediate effect. As I took my school bag, I was confused. What exactly was I going to read? Although I had been the brightest pupil in my primary school, I have never had an independent study for the first time. During our terminal exams, we would only come to class, when it was time for an exam. Our teacher would tell us to detach a piece of paper from our note books. After which, we would keep other things such as our notebooks, school bags, textbooks and so on away from us. Even when we wrote our common entrance and First School Leaving Certificate Examinations, our studies were neither independent nor individualistic one. Our teachers organized extension classes for us.

The only time I had something that looked like an independent study was when I was preparing to represent my school in a quiz competition. The competition was for the best primary four pupils in the whole Imo state. In order to get me prepared for the quiz competition, my teacher gave me a text to read. She also showed me some passages I would memorize. I did the reading and memorizing on my own.However, Aunt Chioma (Mama Matina's daughter) taught me at home. She was a very good teacher; but as Jesus Christ once said "a prophet is not without honor except in his own country, among his own relatives, and in his own house" I never valued her worth. Before I had my dinner each night, she would devote thirty minutes teaching me. This was the routine till the quiz competition was done.

That night, I decided to start my reading with English language. I took my English workbook, and as I was flipping through it, my interest was captured by the assignment we did before our common entrance exam. In that assignment, our teacher told us to fill in certain gaps with verbs. The number one question of the assignment reads thus- Obi ----- rice every day (eat, eats, ate, eaten). In that assignment, I scored ten over ten. And it was the "long good" marked by my teacher with a red pen in that workbook that attracted my attention to that page.

After about ten minutes of my reading, the next place I saw myself was in Mount Horeb. There in

Mount Horeb, I was in my boarding room with other students, with each of us doing different things. I was wearing my day dress and a pair of sandals. I cannot really explain what I was doing in the room. Within few minutes, a bell was ringing; it was time for prep. Together with other students, I ran to the class. Within few minutes, every one of us was busy with his books. While some where reading, others were either drawing or looking at pictures in their text books. The prep lasted for about an hour and thirty minutes. By then, it was miscellaneous time. At this time, one had freedom to do anything one wanted to do. Immediately, I ran into the dormitory, open my cupboard and brought out my beverages. I prepared a cup of tea which I wanted to take with a meat pie I had bought earlier on. As I sat down to start enjoying my meal, what I heard was "Mka, if you are tired of reading, why not go and relax in your bed". Ouch! I was annoyed when I realized that it was all but a dream. I frowningly put back my books in my bag and went to bed. All my dreams that night was about Mount Horeb.

I had spread the news to all my friends that I would soon be a student of Mount Horeb Seminary. Their mood about this development varied. While some where happy with me, others were either jealous or sad.

For the next few days that followed, I was busy reading my books and as well, bragging as if I was already in the school. By Friday, I washed and ironed my primary school uniform. On the eve of my exam day, I went to bed late. I was busy revising my books till around 2:30am. I could not sleep. My mind was ruminating on how I would battle with my exams in the next few hours. It was around 3:00am that I slept. Even at that, my dreams that night were revolving around what I would shortly.

As early as 7:00am, I was ready waiting for dad to dress up. I wore my green short and a yellow shirt which was my primary school uniform. The sandal I was wearing was a new one which Bro Godwin had bought for me at Orieagu Market some days before he travelled to the college. I looked very elegant that day. In a couple of minutes, dad was ready, and we went to where we got a motorcycle that took us to the school. It took us about forty-five minutes to be in Mount Horeb. As I stepped my feet into the school premises, it was as though I had entered heaven. The glory of the institution overwhelmed me. If one thinks that I was engulfed by massive edifices in the school, the person is not far from the truth.

Dad and I went straight to Mr. Anyoha's Office. Mr. Anyoha was the Dean of studies in Mount Horeb. He was a very good friend of dad. As if it was an already made arrangement, the wife came in with two plates of rice. The aroma of the food was enough to wake up a man that was starved to death. Dad took his and ordered me to take mine. Although I did not take the tea mum prepared for me before leaving home I was not hungry.

I knew I may regret not eating the food, but I lost my appetite. I only managed to drink the bottle of Maltina that was served with the rice.Dadate his own food and drinkgracefully as hediscussed with Mr. Anyoha. After about thirty minutes of their chat, Mr. Anyoha told us that it was time to go for accreditation.

We were led to one of the biggest halls in the school Unlike what I had expected, there was great multitude of people than I could imagine. At this point, dad had to leave me to face the drum beat alone. He went to a place reserved for parents and guardians, while I stood with other students. We looked well prepared for the exam. Within some minutes, we were all inside the hall. The examiners kept us waiting for about thirty minutes. It was rumoured that that was when the questions were being set. By 12 noon on the dot, the exam started. When I got my question paper, I first said my prayers as Aunty Harriet taught me.

Aunty Harriet was our Sunday School teacher in St Paul's Extension. We called her Aunty Ocha to describe her complexion. In those days, we took her for a white woman because she was very fair. It was later that I learnt that she was not an Oyibo woman but an albino. In our Sunday School days, Aunty Ocha told us the story of Nehemiah, whom through prayers, worn his master's (the king) sympathy and support to travel home. She also taught us how Master Jesus prayed, and overcame all his challenges.

After my prayers, I opened and answered questions on bible knowledge first, after which, I attempted other questions. The subject that gave me tough time was mathematics. I hated mathematics with passion. But I tried as much I could to subdue it that day. Within thirty minutes I finished answering all the questions and I took my time to go through my work. Being satisfied with what I had done, I said my closing prayers and raised my hand to call the examiner's attention. When he arrived, I submitted my answer script and went out with my shoulders high. At a point, I looked back and discovered that some students were looking at me as if they wanted me to come and help them. Having left the hall, I went straight to where dad was. "That is my son coming" dad told one woman sitting beside him. They were discussing me. As I reached where dad was sitting, the first thing he said was "well done my son". He then asked me how the exam was. I told him "fine". He shook me and said "I know you have given them an assignment. By the time they will finish marking the assignment, they will know that you are my son". He then took me to the school canteen and bought me meat pie and fanta. As I was eating the snacks, my mind flashed back to the delicious meal I missed in Mr. Anyoha's house. I wished to go back for it, but then, it was too late.

As I was coming out from the canteen, I heard noises that seeded to emanate from the exam hall. My colleagues were just submitting their scripts. Before long, the compound was filled with students. They were all moving towards one direction. It was the school refectory. It was announced in the hall that we all should go to the school refectory for refreshment.

For over two weeks, I was waiting with eagerness to hear that our result was out, but to no avail. I was in church service one Sunday. It was time for announcement, the priest had stressed on everything in the bulletin. He then brought out an envelope from his Ekpere Na Abu. My attention was captured when he read the headline of the letter. It was a letter from Mount Horeb Seminary. Although I gave him all my attention, I never understood what he was reading. The only thing I understood was that the result of the common entrance exam was out; and that attracted more of my attention. At that point, it was as if I was dreaming. He further mentioned the resumption date. The last thing he did was to call the names of those from our parish who gained admission into the prestigious institution. My name was among the ones called. As soon as I heard my name, I became shy immediately a voice shouted "Praaaise the lord!", the congregation responded alleluia. It was mum who led the shout of joy. She started scrambling for me, but I could not show up as all eyes were on me. Mum immediately located and carried me up. The congregation started cheering me. During all these happenings, dad only smiled and showed no other concern over what was going on. I left church that day as the happiest person. I walked home with my friends and younger ones. We were discussing nothing but how my life in the dormitory would look like. I narrated to them how I would spend each single day in my new school. At home, people were coming to congratulate me as if I had received a ticket to heaven. Our compound was the center of attention for the village that day. But I had no time for elderly people. My whole attentions was given to my peers whom I had started missing. In my bed, I dreamt about Mount Horeb, its dormitory, field, classroom, refectory and so on.

I barely had a week to pack to my new environment. All I needed to live in the dormitory was ready. Dad and mum had bought me even things I had never expected they would buy for me. But one thing was wanting. By Friday that predated my day of departure, I had never seen my school uniform, sandals and belt. Although these things were not in the prospectus I thought they were omitted because the school authorities knew that a student must come to school with such necessary things. I never asked for my uniforms because I knew dad was full of surprises. He may have ordered our family tailor to sew one for me as the tailor had the sizes of dresses we could wear. On that Friday, all my friends assembled in my house. We all knew we may not see ourselves for long after that evening. It was then that I remembered that I would not have time to go to Dimeke to fetch water, Ikpanta to fetch fire wood, Mbara to pluck Icheku, Udara, Ube and so on with my friends. Another thing that caught my emotion most was that I would have limited time for Sunday school and junior choir again. As these thoughts were running through my mind, I started wishing that the resumption date could be extended.

It was Saturday. As early as 7am, our compound was filled up again. This time around, it was not only by my friends. Both my Sunday School members and my Sunday School teachers were there. They had gathered in the church compound for Oru-Ogige, when Aunty Ocha remembered that I had told her that I would be going to school that day. I guess it was my absence from the work that reminded her of my journey. It was unlike me to be absent in both choir practice, compound cleaning and any other church activity. Before their arrival, I was already prepared. Dad had earlier announced that he would take me to school before 7:30am so that he could meet up with the rest of his appointments. Immediately I saw my gang, tears started gushing out of my eyes. I knew it would take a long time to be in their company again. That Saturday's Oru-Ogige was done in my house. They helped in loading my luggage into a pick-up van dad has hired for that purpose. Before long, everything was ready. They had also prayed for my wellbeing in the dormitory. The driver had started the car and was waiting for me to come in so that we could take off, but I was nowhere to be found.

During the prayers, when all eyes were closed, I had run to our neighbour's house. I never wanted to go to Mount Horeb again; I could not imagine staying in a lonely hall, reading, and playing with unknown people when my friends were there in my village. All the adults around started searching for me, but none of my friends was willing to join them in the search. I guess their prayer was for me not to be seen. By 8:30am, I was still nowhere to be found. It was then that Aunty Ocha shouted my name, I wanted not to respond, but I could not withhold myself from answering my beloved teacher, mentor and model. I reluctantly answered and she said with a shaky voice "nwoke obi-oma bia". From the sound of her voice, I knew she had already started missing me. I left my hideout to answer her. Dad was very annoyed with me because I had wasted his time. He wanted to flog me, but mum and Aunty Ocha intervened. Aunty Ocha took me by my hand and handed over to me Our Daily and a Revised Standard Version of the holy Bible the Sunday school children had bought for me. She then pecked me and led me into the pickup-van.

The death of a youth had never caused the weeping that took place in my compound that day. As the car moved, every one of us except dad was crying.

Within about 45 minutes of our journey, I neither talked to dad nor looked him in his face. I was thinking that he did me bad, for at least, he would have postponed the journey to Monday.

In a moment we were at Mount Horeb. The van was parked under one umbrella tree in the school compound. I was still in the car when dad left for Mr. Anyoha's house. On his returning, two men were following him. They were two among the school's security personnel. The two men carried my entire luggage at once. These were things that took my peers (about 25 of them) time to load in the car. I hated the men, because for me, I thought that offloading will take us time, thereby extending the time I would have to stay with dad before his departure. As they were carrying my properties, they asked dad my level, when he answered; they told him that I would stay in White Dormitory. White Dormitory was meant for first year students. It was one of the best dormitories in the institution. On getting to the dormitory, I was the only student who had returned back to school. After arranging my properties for me, dad sat me on my bed. I have been moody all these while. I did not greet the security men when they came to carry my bags, not to talk of thanking them for helping me in carrying them. He asked me to cheer up that he loved me. He said he was doing the best for me because that was what he owed me as a father. He continued by advising me to put in my best in my academics so as to make him proud. After series of advice, he dipped his hands into his pocket and brought out #100. He told me to use the money over the weekend, and that whenever I needed something, I should go to Mr. Anyoha's house. That made me angrier.

I expected him to give me at least #1000. I never knew that he had dropped #2000 with Mr. Anyoha for me. After then, he stood up, pecked me and left.

I felt desolated that day. The whole hall that could accommodate up to one hundred students was all mine. I remembered Mum, Aunty Ocha, my siblings, and my friends. Like the flowing Atlantic, tears were flowing through my cheek. I had no one to console me. It was only me and my world. I ran towards the window, peep through it, expecting to see dad, but not even his shadow was anywhere to be seen. I walked back slowly (as though I was pleading with the floor to walk on it) to my bed. I sat there and agonized for about an hour. I never knew when I slept off. I dreamt of where I was playing with some boys of my age, though I did not know whom the boys were. At a point in that dream, Emeka, one of my best friends in the village came and asked me whom the boys I was playing with were. He further told me that he hated what I and my dad did. "What did we do?" I asked him. He queried me back "why did you enter the pickup van with our football...? And now you are playing with other boys while we were at home waiting for you." As soon as he said that, he started crying and ran away. Then I woke up. I needed no Joseph to interpret my dreams for me. I knew that my friends at home were missing me the same way I was missing them. I sat on my bed. I could not cry again because I was tired of crying having cried from home through my journey to Mount Horeb.

Another thing that made me to withheld my emotions was the arrival of another student. I did not know the exact time the lad and his mum arrived, that was when I was sleeping. I later learnt that the mother was still there because the boy had refused her going back home. He had been weeping. I was a bit elder than him in our new home. "Ngwa biazie ka anyi lawa" said the mum. Both of them left the dormitory. At that point, I was extremely disappointed in my father. I wished it was mum that brought me to school. I nearly cursed dad at that point. The mother and son went out. I never knew that it was a ruse employed by the woman to get her son seized by the security while she left. It was all a surprise for the boy when he was held by the same men who carried my bags. The boy nearly vomited his tongue as he was shouting on top of his voice. That incident made me happy. I was happy that the boy did not leave with his mother; at least, I had a corner mate. On the other hand, I was annoyed with those security men who derived pleasure in seizing other people's children. The boy was later led into the dormitory by the security men who threaten to flog him if he fails to keep quiet.

The boy remained calm for a while. After about thirty minutes, he disappeared. When the security men asked me after his way about, I damned them because I was seeing them as my enemies.

It was not until 5:30pm that students started trooping back. Before long, the school compound was filled up with both returning students and freshmen. Seeing others made me to comfort I had people to spend the night with. By 8pm, people were still coming back. There was no power supply that night, but the school generator gave us light. Around 9pm, a short, fair man came into our dormitory. In his introduction, he told us that his name was Mr. Theodore Mbadinuju, but he urged us to address him as "Mr T". He said that he was the hall master. He advised us to see him as father, friend, brother, roommate and teacher. He promised to provide us with all we needed, ranging from protection, advice and so on. He told us many things that night, but I was not eager to listen to his stories. After his advice, he ordered us to go down to the school refectory for our dinner. None of us in my dormitory gave attention to the food. We all had lost appetite.

In the next few minutes, a bell rang but we did not know what could make them ring bell at that time. During my primary school days, bells only ringduring assembly time, time to change lectures, break time, dismissal time and may be when there was need for impromptu gathering. We were lost at the sound of the bell. Shortly, Mr. T came in again. He told us that it was time for lights out. I did not know what he meant by lights out. He further told us to put on our pajamas and lie down.

As l lay in my bed, I recalled all that happened during the day, from the time my friends visited me at home to the time Mr. T addressed us. I looked at the bed next to mine, there was no one lying in it. It belonged to the guy that came after me, the one that wanted to go with the mother. I found it difficult to sleep that night. Fortunately for me, I did not know when I dozed off.

At about 6 am the following day, Mr. T was in my dormitory. They had rung the bell for about one hour ago. But we could not wake up. He was surprised we were still sleeping having told us last night that at the sound of the bell, we should come out with our buckets to take our bath. He took his time going from one bed to the other waking us up. He showed us where to fetch water for bathi. We did not eat that morning. Mr. T had told us that we use Sundays for fasting. Before we finished taking our bath, the school social prefect had dropped a pair of white trouser; a pair of white shoes, white stocking and white shirt on our beds. We were told that the dresses were ours and that we should only wear them on Sundays for service. Before 9am, we had all appeared in our white like angels. The service took place in the school chapel and by 10:30am, it was over. We stayed indoors till around 2pm when the bell sounded. It was the same bell, but not the normal sound we used to hear. It was when we saw old students going to the refectory that we realized that the bell was for lunch. We joined the chorus. After the meal, we had our siesta. By 5pm, we were summoned for evening worship which lasted for an hour.

As l was going to the dormitory, l saw a woman approaching with a boy. They first went to Uncle T's house. His house was close to the school gate, the first house one could see after the security office at the gate. It was that boy that disappeared the previous day. The mother narrated to Uncle T how he refused to stay the previous day. She said that when she left her son in school, she went straight to market, but was astonished to discover on arrival that her son was at home. He sneaked out without the knowledge of the security men. She handed the lad to Mr. T who promised her that her son would be taken care of.

It was my first Monday in the school. The rising bell was rung around 4:30am. Through the help of the chapel prefect, we woke earlier than the previous day. All movements were toward the school chapel. We were going for morning devotion. The devotion lasted for about 30 minutes and we went to our classes. It was as if we were all forced to abide by the routine. Of course, we were, because none of us was willing to leave his bed in the first instance. There in the class, the study prefect had told us to pick up a book and read. But his words left the class with him as soon as he turned his back to leave us. We all bent down our heads and in a moment began to snore. It was around 5:30am when we heard the sound of a bell that we woke up. This time around, we deserved some credits. At least, we were able to rise at the sound of the bell. We all took our lantern and went straight to the dormitory. We knew it was time to take our baths, so we took our buckets to the school underground tank. I was thinking that we would be given hot water to dilute the cold one, but that was a wishful thinking. I was not used to bathing with cold water. Although I managed it the previous day, I thought that it happened that way because we were late to the bathroom. As soon as I was given the cold water, I remembered home, I remembered mum too. Mum could not allow me to take my bath with cold water alone. Having no other option, I hurriedly took my bath with the water and ran into the dormitory. As I was taking my bath, I was thinking about which cloth to wear. Dad did not sew me school uniform, but he had advised me to take along with me my primary school uniform. I was relieved when the senior prefect visited and announced "we the school authorities are sorry that your uniforms are not yet ready. Bear with us..." He further advised us to wear our primary school uniforms. Within few minutes after his address, the bell rang again. We did not know what it was calling for.

This time around, it was the sanitary prefect that came to our room and urged us to take our brooms and go outside. He said it was time for morning functions. We gathered together with older students. We were more than 200, but I was still lonely in the midst of such multitude. The only person I could have known was Ikechi, but he was no more in Mount Horeb. He had gone to Port Harcourt to live with his parents. The sanitary prefect partitioned the school premises into portions, with some numbers of students to sweep them. We were six in my own group with all of us from the same dormitory.

Within fifteen minutes, the morning function was over and we retired to our various rooms to prepare for morning assembly. The assembly ground was in front of the staff room. Apart from JSS1 student, others appeared in their school uniforms, well ironed. The morning assembly was conducted by Mr. Ibe, the Vice-principal. He was a short dark man from Umuowo. After the national and school anthems, he delved into announcement. Among the things he did, was the recognition and welcoming of freshmen. He gave us an orientation about the school ethics; and admonished us to be good students of the institution. He strictly warned the old students not to bully us. He reminded them that a tree was once an embryo. Finally, he promised that our uniforms would be ready before the weekend. After the assembly, we retired to the refectory for our breakfast. It was a meal of yam porridge. I managed to eat mine because it was neither hot nor delicious. To worsen the matter, the meal was very meager. Others were eating theirs, so I managed to eat mine.

Before 8:30am, everyone was in class. The first lecture that day was Igbo language. The teacher was Mrs. Flora Mbadinuju, Mr. T's wife. She was a kind woman and an opposite of what I used to see in primary school. Notwithstanding that she was teaching lgbo, she was speaking English to us. The first thing she did was to lead the class on a marathon self-introduction. It was then I learnt the names of some of my class mates. One of the names I heard for the first time that day was Osungwu. For me, the name seemed very strange. Any way, it was the best name for the bearer. The bearer was the stubborn dude who had played on the intelligence of our security men and went home the day her mother brought him to school.

We had eight lectures that day and classes ended around 2pm. We used 30 minutes for lunch, an hour for siesta, then we retired to class for evening classes. The evening class lasted till 3:45pm. We then had to do other chores before the day folded.

That was exactly how our days in Mount Horeb were. The major changes in those routines were on Thursdays when we had sports instead of evening classes

The days I enjoyed most was the second Saturdays of the month. That was our visiting days. Morning function began very early. We would clean every nook and cranny of the school because of our visiting parents, guardians, friends and well-wishers. The visiting started by 10am. Each visitor would stay under the big umbrella tree in front of Mr. T's house with the person visited. One could spend any number of hours with his visitor until 6:30pm. The nights of visiting days were to us Christmas. There would be more food to eat than those that would eat them. Parents also used the opportunity to bombard their wards with beverages, and pocket monies. But one obvious thing about this visiting was that the junior students were the most visited; may be the senior ones were seen as old enough to take care of themselves. Senior students frequently exploited the younger ones of their beverages. One of the notorious of the seniors then was Senior Ocean. This was a nick name which portrayed that he was too deep to be filled. As such, any day he remembered the junior students, a very large number of them would give him their snacks, provisions, pocket monies and so on. Senior Ocean would always call out any of his preys, ask him to reciteThe Lord is My Shepherd in the Igbo language. His target would always be the line that says "I shall not want" In the Igbo language, it says "odighi ihe korom" which literally translate to "I lack nothing". Once the students says "odighi ihe korom", Senior Ocean would ask him to pause. He would ask the student if he truly meant that he lacked nothing. He would start enumerating "do you mean you lack no biscuit, milk, milo, sugar? Ok me, I lack all these things. Now take my cup and make it to overflow as yours would always do" The junior student would need no prophet to interpret to him that the senior meant that he should give him biscuit, milk, milo, and sugar.

One academic year had pass. I was then in JSS2. At the dawn of the term, SS2 students were empowered.

Senior George became our new Senior Prefect. He was from Umueze. Senior George fetched his fame through intelligence and hardwork. Even when he was in SS1, our teachers would always refer to him whenever they advised us on hardworking and self-dependence in studies. When they-SS2 students were acting on interim, Senior George would always come to our class to either teach us literature, use of English or some other things he may deem necessary. He told us that he was working on a book. This motivated us tremendously. Almost all of us then bought sixty leaves exercise book to start up our own writing. We also had another separate exercise book where we wrote any new word we came across.

Although it was known that Senior George was the most intelligent student in the school, we were not convinced that he would be the senior prefect. We were thinking that it would go to senior Ikembono. This we thought because he was more masculine than the tiny Senior George who always felt sick. Another advantage senior Ikembono had over Senior George was that he was from Umuowo. Thus, a brother to both Mr. T and Mr. Ibe the Vice-principal.

During his tenure as the senior prefect, Senior George carried out many reformations in the school. Some of the things he did were to give our social night a new colour. It was a social gathering of the students every last Saturday of the month. During the gathering, each class was expected to present a drama. But when Senior

George took over student's administration, he made it compulsory for each class to add both presentation of poems and any other talent that one would want to showcase. To make the social night more competitive, he introduced the idea of presenting gift to the best class that performed. "Freedom" was also given to five best performers in the whole school. If one was under this award of freedom, the person would not participate in morning function, washing of the school lavatories. The person had free water for bathing from the school water tank, a lion share in the refectory. And most importantly, he would not be bullied by any senior till the next social night. This award of freedom made our social night very enticing because everyone did put in his best to win it.

Another important reformation carried out by this regime was the introduction of Press club and Jet club. While press club was for art students, Jet was for science students. I belonged to press club which was headed by the senior prefect. Through his reforms especially in art and literature, the school was made famous outside. No school was able to defeat us in drama, debate, quiz and generally all social and cultural activities.

As usual, the first few weeks of this administration was aggressive in nature. Although the administrators knew their onus, they were epitome of tyrants. Mount Horeb was under the reign of Terror. No one could question the authorities of our then Stalinist Senior George and his comrades. The one that surprised everyone most was our loved Senior George He had changed drastically. It was then I realized that truly, power corrupts. Senior George would come into our class, blew big grammars to us expecting us to reply. But how could we reply what we did not understand? Running out of patience, he would order us to be on our knees. He would walk out shakily as if breeze was about to blow his tiny body away. In the next few minutes, he would reappear with numerous whips. He would mount our desks and give us general flogging.

One day, we were annoyed by the maltreatment. We wrote a letter to be submitted to Mr. T. where we requested that Senior George and his cohorts be questioned. We did not know how the senior got the news. He came to our class; "petition writers!" he screamed. We looked around waiting for petition writers to answer him. We thought that was someone's name. It was later that we learnt that the letter we wrote was called petition. He did not flog us for the petition. Rather he congratulated us for the legendary move we made. We thought he was saying the opposite. We did not know he meant it as he told us that it was wise for one to follow due process to pursue their rights. Writing the petition, he said showed him that we know how best to go about what we thought was our rights. He ordered our class prefect: Nwike Chimere to produce a copy of the petition. When this was done, he took chalk and corrected us on how best to write petition and other formal letters we may want to write subsequently.

From that day, we became his friend. He took his time to teach and explain anything that we found difficult to understand. It was then that we realized that being a bully was not part of his life. Rather, having no physical strength, and being seen by others as a weakling, he decided to use his authority to defend himself, and to avert intimidation.

In my third year, our principal was changed. Venerable Rollins Elu who was both our principal and the administrator of ST Augustine Anglican Church Umuala had been replaced with Rev. Caiaphas Okeh. Rev. Caiaphas was a very vibrant man in his late thirties. Because of how strict he was to both senior students and teachers, he was christened Stone Code. We heard a breath of fresh air during his regime as penalties ranging from expulsion, suspension, clearing of grasses and so on were imposed based on the level of offence one committed.

Before students, Stone Code had little interest in his work as a pastor because he spent most of his time in the seminary. He would always wear sports attire when coming to inspect us. One day, Senior Collins popularly known as Currency was whipping us because we did not fetch water for him when we were fetching water for the kitchen. Unfortunately for him, Stone

Code was coming to inspect us that day. "Young man why are you flogging those boys" he asked with a voice that roared like a thunder. The senior was speechless because we were innocent. "Can any of you tell me why you are being punished?" He asked us. I raised up my hand and explained exactly why we were being flogged. He ordered Currency to be on his knees, but the senior ran away. He was told through the senior prefect not to return to school again except with either of his parents. The following day, Senior Collins was in school with one old man. Two of them went to the principal's office; and had an undertaking letter signed. It was later that the news circulated that the man that had stood as Collins's referee was not his father. He had gone to Isinweke, arranged with a motorcycle commercial rider whom he promised to pay his daily wage if he could stand before our principal as his father. The man played his role perfectly well before the principal.

That particular incident placed me in a tight corner throughout my stay in Mount Horeb. Being the one that exposed Collins before Stone Code, all the senior students in the school hated me with passion. They remarked my plate; thus, during meal, I would have the smallest of the food. In terms of clean up, my name would always appear among those that would wash the lavatories. Washing school toilet then was a death sentence because that place used to be very filthy with maggots dancing on excreta.

When I discovered that things were not smiling for me at all, I decided to tell dad that I would like to change school. I did not tell him what my reasons were, but I have made up my mind. He encouraged me to wait till after my Junior Secondary Certificate Examination. By May that year, we were done with our exams; and off I went and never to return to Mount Horeb again as a student.

Yours faithful son in the lord,
Mka

## CHAPTER FOUR

# LIFE IN LAGOS

**THREE YEARS** have passed since Mka left the seminary. He finished his SSCE exams in July, 2009. He wanted to continue his education but things were no longer smooth for him. His father was not financially buoyant anymore to sponsor him through the University education. More so, he had nine siblings, who needed to pass through primary and secondary educations. So, sending Mka to the university would be tantamount to withdrawing others from both secondary and primary schools. Sequel to that, an arrangement has to be made for Mka to go and learn either a handiwork or a trade in the city. But to him, learning a handiwork was never in his personal plan, but for the fact that it had to be in the city, that was manageable for him. He saw it as an opportunity to travel out of Imo State. Mka had spent all his life time so far in the village. It was only two times that he travelled out of the state. The first time was in the year 2007, when he represented his diocese in a national youth conference. The second time Mka left Imo state was in the year 2008. When he went as a children's teacher to Anglican national conference at Abuja, so to leave Imo state was a great opportunity for Mka. This time around, he was not going as a churchman spend only a weekend in a township church premises, but as a grownup to live for a very long period in the city in search of greener pasture.

He was to travel to Lagos to live with his father's friend; Mr. Peter. Mr. Peter was a businessman from Oyo state but lived in Lagos. He met with Odu in Kaduna some years back before Mka was born. They have been very good friends though they have not seen for a very long time. Mr. Peter decided to live without marrying because he felt that marriage was a smoother. He sold food ingredients in Boundary Market, Lagos. He was indeed successful in his business. He had earlier told Mka's father that he needed an honest boy who would learn the trade from him. As such, Mka's father concluded arrangement with him for his son to be the needed apprentice.

At about 5:30pm, Mka looked out of the bus window and was overwhelmed by what he saw. The signboard that read "THIS IS LAGOS" gave him the satisfaction that he has finally entered the crowded city where only the fittest survive. He started calculating how his days in Lagos would be, how he would be a good boy to his master, how he would make money within the shortest possible time and go back to school. All these thoughts never left him till when the driver got to Mazamaza. That was a place Mka's father had told the driver to drop him. Mka brought out a phone number given to him by his father; it was Mr. Peter's contact. He approached a nearby business centre and gave them the line to dial. He has never touched a cell phone for once not to talk of making calls with them. That day was the first opportunity for him. To him, Lagos has already started giving him access and opportunity to things he has never done before. "Omo take the phone, person don pick your call" Mka delightfully collected the phone from the lady and spoke with Mr. Peter. He gave him the description of where he was standing and Mr. Peter told him to wait for him for a while.

For more than thirty minutes, Mka was still waiting patiently for Mr. Peter. Though he tarried, Mka could not feel that. The poor boy was busy admiring the beauty of Lagos state while calculating how his life would be in his new city. Mka's mind roamed through the whole city of Lagos that day. He also within 30 minutes' time has illusorily lived for more than ten years in Lagos where he became a very successful man. At the climax of his psychic rumination, a man touched him. It was Mr. Peter. "You are Mka; am I right?" asked the man. When Mka responded in agreement, he shook his hands and said, "Welcome to Lagos. I hope your journey was less stressful. Oya come let us go to the house so that you can rest". They immediately boarded a taxi and drove to Mr. Peter's house.

"Eka-abo" was the greetings received by Mr. Peter on getting to his house. It was his younger brother: Tolu that greeted as he rushed to ease Mr. Peter and Mka of the loads they were carrying. Tolu was Mr. Peter's younger brother of about twenty-five years. He is very dark in complexion and chubby. He was to be Mka's friend and guardian through the latter's stay in Lagos. Immediately, Tolu brought out a small tiger generator and put it on. There was no power supply in their street that night. Mka was impressed with what he saw. Mr. Peter lived in one room in a public yard. The room was filled with few loads but because the one room contained all their belongings, it looked so filled up. Tolu led Mka to the public lavatory to freshen up. After his shower, he had his dinner and they went to bed. In Mr. Peter's house, praying before going to bed was never in their agenda. Mka had wanted to ask for that, but he was somewhat shy.

At about 4:00am the following day, Tolu woke Mka up to inform him that it was time to go to the market. This was a very big surprise for Mka. He was used to waking up on time, but not that too early. The journey of the previous day got him very tired. But he had no option; he had to give in to what he came for. As he was led by Tolu to wash his face before they could set off, Mr. Peter intervened by telling Tolu to go alone. He said he would come along with Mka later. That was a good news for Mka. He then had to go back to bed. It was about 7:30 am that Mr. Peter woke up and got ready for the day's business. They entered a Keke-Napep that took them to Boundary Market. It was indeed a very large market with thousand and one people trooping in and out. Mr. Peter led Mka to his shop and left never to return till around 5pm that day. "You chop for house before coming to market? Tolu asked Mka who replied no. He bought ewa-agonyi and bread for Mka. That was the first time Mka was eating such combination of food.

Mka was really surprised with the whole thing he was seeing in Boundary Market: for the first time he saw petrol engines grinding egusi, ogbono, pepper and so on. Again, the rate at which buyers were trooping and buying puzzled him. To him, one could make up to fifty thousand naira a day. But to his greatest surprise, at about 10am, it was as if buyers were told not to come again. Sounds of grinding engines could sparsely be heard again. This surprised Mka, but he could neither talk nor ask question over that. At about 2pm, Tolu went out and came back with a plate of rice and plantain. "Come make we chop", he told Mka. Mka had wanted to eat, but for the fact that both of them would eat from the same plate, he replied that he was not hungry. He was indeed shy of eating with Tolu whom he has known nothing about. Tolu ate the food without uttering any other word to Mka. Towards 3pm, buyers started coming again. At about 6:30 PM, the shop was closed and the boys left.

Mka had stayed for two months with Tolu being his closest associate. He was fast learning the marketing strategy. His honesty made both Tolu and Mr. Peter to trust him so much. He was more or less the treasurer of the business. But even in the face of all these, Mka was yet to derive joy from the business. All he had wanted was to continue his education. As such, his major distraction from the trade was his books. He had taken many novels and some textbooks along with him to Lagos. He used any single second that came around him to read.

Mka has given Tolu some relieve. Knowing that Mka can handle the shop alone, he usually left the shop for him after early morning market to God knows where. He would stay there for more than two hours. What always confused Mka was that Tolu always came back looking famished. He warned Mka not to tell Mr. Peter of his movement. One day, Mr. Peter visited the shop at around 12 noon and Tolu was not around and Mka was busy reading the book, "Tough Time Never Lasts, But Tough People Do". It was as if Robert Schuller; the author had Mka in mind when he gave the book the title. Mka was lost in the book when Mr. Peter came in, such that he could not notice the presence of anybody. For up to ten minutes Mr. Peter stayed in the shop, Mka could not decipher that his Oga was around. Mr Peter angrily left without dropping any word.

The shop closed around 7pm that day. On getting to the house, Tolu and Mka discovered that Mr. Peter had brought out two whips. That was the first time Mka would see such in the house. But Tolu knew that something was absolutely wrong somewhere. He called Mka outside and asked "Oga come shop today that time wey I comot?" No, replied Mka. "Talk true, you comot that time wey I no dey shop"? asked Tolu again. "No" replied Mka. "The reason why I dey ask na because yawa don ghast, that bullala wey dey inside room na for us. Oga go chop our yansh today with the cane. See, if em flog you cry well well ooo because if you do big boi na em be say em go continue dey flog until you cry. Na so I deey do whenever em flog me". The whole thing was sounding illusional to Mka who was imagining why they should be flogged. Before long, Mr. Peter came in and ordered the boys to be on their knees. "Tolu where you go when I come shop today", he asked, but Tolu could not say anything because he knew that answering the question would amount to wasting time because the truth was that he would be flogged that night. "No be you I dey ask?" he repeated in a louder voice. "I no go anywhere" replied Tolu "so you mean say I no dey see road again abi? I don become mad man wey dey talk anyhow. Abi na accusation I dey accuse untop your head say you comot when I come for shop? And for you, wetin dem dey call you Soyimka abi na wetin?, wetin you think say carry you come Lagos? To dey read like mad man abi na to learn business? I come shop today, stay for a long time, you no even notice say I dey there talkless of greeting me. You think say na library you dey? And I believe say na so una dey pursue my customers with una I don kia attitudes".

That night, he not only flogged the boys mercilessly, but denied them dinner. To Mka, he warned him not to read again throughout his stay with him. He also warned him to learn how to communicate with dictions people could understand not speaking "big big grammars" that scare customers away. It was indeed a bitter night for the two boys, but it created a bond between them. Tolu vowed that he would play back on Mr. Peter. As such, the following morning, the boys left for shop earlier than they have ever done. As early as 3:30am, the boys were already good to leave for the shop. That morning, there was no Keke-Napep to convey them to the market. It was too early indeed. They had to trek to the market. On their way, a group of three boys and a girl approached and asked them where they were going by that time of the day. Before they could utter a word, they were apprehended and taken to a corner where they were ransacked and the whole money they were taking to shop as change, were taken from them. As if that was not enough, the boys asked them why they were not with any girl. Before Tolu could try to utter a word, he was given the heaviest slap he has ever received. One of the boys then advised the girl in their midst to do her "business". The girl immediately stripped Mka, brought out his innocent vein that was as flat as withered Ugu in a hot afternoon. The girl tried as much as she could to get the vein erect for "her business" to be done, but it was a futile one. In order to punish Mka, she took a broom stick and pierced it into his urinary. It was then Tolu's turn. But like Mka's vein, Tolu's could not respond. One of the boys became very angry and had to give Tolu the anal sex of his life before they flee. The two boys who were already suffering the punishment given to them by their boss the previous night felt the whole world was against them that morning. They could not get to their shop till around 10am. Irrespective of the pains, Tolu warned Mka not to tell anyone what had happened. That day, they could not sale much. But they were less concerned about the bad market. To them, it was all caused by their Oga who denied them food the previous night. Even in the face of the poor sales, Tolu had to spend up Two Thousand Naira on their feeding that day.

The following Saturday was to be like Christmas for the boys. There would be no market that day. The Union of Egusi Traders would be travelling to Benue State for the burial of one of their members. So it was a free day for the boys. For the first time since Mka's came to Lagos he would stay at home for the whole day. After washing Mr. Peter's dirty clothes and clean up exercise, Tolu told Mka that they would enjoy themselves for the whole weekend as their boss would not return till the following week. He further asked Mka what he liked most, drink, sex, food or what? He assured Mka that he should just name his choice and he would make it available for him. Mka was very confused by the question. He could not answer anything. Before long, there was a knock at their door. "enter" said Tolu. Two girls of about the same age appeared. They were prostitutes in their early twenties. They were dressed in such a way that their cleavages could clearly be seen with a very short skirt. One of them walked straight to Tolu and started caressing him. The touches were so tense that Tolu immediately fell on the bed for "the business" of the day to be carried out. The other lady went to Mka, but like the biblical Joseph in the escapable trap of Mrs. Potiphar, Mka ran out from the room. Having left the room, the door was locked from inside as the two girls faced Tolu. The groan was so tense that neighbors knew what was going on. But nobody could utter a word. It was a routine. Mr. Peter was not exceptional. He changed women like one changes clothes on daily basis.

Mka could not go anywhere. He was just standing outside leaving his mind to do his own sex. At a point, he went close to the window to peep. Though he could not see anything happening inside, his mind was seeing everything. If only Tolu's vein was as stiff as Mka's was, the two ladies could have had their cubicles torn that very day. It was after one hour that the ladies came out. As they were leaving, they were counting some cash. It was their wage from Tolu. When Mka opened the door, he realized that Tolu was deeply asleep. When Tolu finally got up, his gestures showed that the whole pain he was passing through since the night they were starved to bed were all over. He was so cheerful with Mka but chided him for his amateur behavior before the whores he brought. He has concluded to coach and make it up for Mka before their Oga could come back. Achieving this aim would serve him two purposes: Mka would not have the boldness to confess what has happened to their boss when he comes back. Secondly, he needed Mka to be a good partner in crime. With this plan in mind, Tolu asked Mka the last time he had sex. It was indeed a very costly question for Mka to answer. To him, it was abnormal for a boy of his age to be involved in that kind of discussion. He tried to rebuff the question, but Tolu who was smarter and more exposed than him repeated the question. "I have never done that before" Mka reluctantly said. Tolu was not all that surprised to hear that because through his naïve attitudes, Mka has shown that he is still "JJC", Tolu then concluded that he has to do something about that before long. He did not talk about sex to Mka again. The following day which was Sunday, Tolu told Mka that they would be attending a friend's birthday party. Mka was happy to hear that. He has heard that lots of party activities happen in Lagos. The Yoruba people, he heard cannot live for a week without partying. But he has not witnessed any of such since he went to Lagos. To him, that would be the first time he would attend a party. The two boys have taken their bath as Mka ran to his bag to get his previous year's Christmas clothe for the party. It was an up and down brocade dress sewn by Mr. Chicago; one of the best tailors in Orieagu Market. But before he could found it, Tolu threw a black bag to him. It contained a pair of trouser and a T shirt. Mka was surprised to see that. He never knew that Tolu has been keeping the clothes in the same room where they have been staying with their boss without any other person knowing that. To Mka, for Tolu to have skillfully planned and executed the plan to that extent, he really proved that he was the master of the house. Without any question, Mka who was fast responding to his coach wore the new dress and they went out for the party.

At exactly 9:30 pm, the MC took over the stage. The party had commenced. People were trooping in and out, both males and females alike. The whole thing was new to Mka. But he has decided not to "fall Tolu's hands" as the later has earlier warned him. The celebrant; Amina was called upon to cut the birthday cake. Amina was the only daughter of Alhaji Mustafa; a wealthy Muslim cleric who was also a businessman in the Boundary Market.

She was celebrating her 19th birthday. She was very tall and dark in complexion. Amina met Mka for the first time in the market the day she went to her father's shop. Although she exchanged no words with Mka who did not take cognizance of her presence in the market that day. But since then she has hardly spent a day without having the thought of Mka taking a reasonable chunk of her time. As such, seeing Mka in her birthday party was the greatest gift she received that day. Without much concern about how he managed to come, she concluded that it was Tolu that came alongside with him. After cutting the cake, she was called upon to come out to the stage to dance with her boyfriend. It was indeed embarrassing to the invitees to know that as beautiful and popular Amina was in the whole vicinity, she had no boyfriend to dance with. Of a truth, she has not been in relationship before, though she has had many admirers and male friends. When the MC discovered that Amina was serious that he has no boy of her own to dance with, he threatened her that the cake would not be eaten till Amina picks any boy in the party hall to dance with. Everyone present with a vein under his trousers was signaling her to point at them so that they would dance together. Some even went as far as spreading money on her to lobby her; but she could not give in to any of them. Mka was busy observing and smiling as the whole event was going on. To him, Amina having no boyfriend is a normal thing. She was not corrupt from Mka's calculations and parameter.

Unknowingly for Mka, Amina who was always looking at Mka's direction saw him smiling. She mistook his smiles for a green light. She then took a bold step and walked straight to him, pecked him on the forehead and bid him to join him on the stage for a dance. The peck sent a hot signal down to Mka's marrows. He felt lost and did not know what to do. He has liked Amina whom he has discovered was a good girl for not having a boyfriend. As such, the damsel ought not to be disappointed. But on the contrary, Aunty Ocha has told the story of how John the Baptist was murdered as the result of a lady's dance during Herod's birthday. From the story, Mka has concluded that party dancing is a sin. As this whole Third World War was raging in his mind, he got a tap from Tolu who signaled him to join Amina on the stage. Mka had to bury his conscience not because of Tolu's tap, but because of the embarrassment Amina would face. He did not want the poor girl to be disappointed in him. He did not want her guests to go without eating her birthday cake as the MC threatened. He finally joined Amina. But the mess of the whole show was that Mka never went close to Amina during the dance. Even when Amina wanted to rock him, he moved some inches away. More so, the whole disappointment came with Mka's dance step. He was busy dancing Igbo cultural dance while the DJ was playing a classical pop song. But then, the whole thing was that people could eat Amina's cake because a boy danced with her during her birthday party. After about five minutes of the dance between Amina and Mka, the floor was then opened for everyone to rock it over with their friends. From that moment, no one saw Amina for the rest of the party. She left embarrassed. To her, she could have met Mka before that day and gotten him ready for the show. But, then, she never wanted to tell him how she was feeling about him. So seeing Mka was then an avenue for her to publicly show him that he was the man her heart has finally found rest with. On his own side, Mka was a bit relieved for saving Amina. To him, he has done his own dancing. So the stage should be taken over by those who were yet to do theirs. He was busy watching and condemning most of the girls who were allowing boys like Tolu to dance very close with them.

After the party at about 12:50am, Amina reappeared to thank her guests for honoring her invitation. She publicly gave special thanks to Mka whom she addressed as her best friend. Immediately after the appreciation, she went and whispered something to Tolu. By then people have started going, but Tolu; because of what Amina whispered to him was not making any move; Mka remained calm as he was told by Tolu that they would leave in few minutes' time. When everyone has left the party hall, Amina came out from where she was sitting. Immediately Tolu saw her, he excused himself. Tolu was not a child in that kind of game; He excused himself through what they called "Exilic Banishment", a process whereby someone leaves a particular scene for their friend when the latter's lover arrives. The large party hall was then deserted except Mka and Amina. Amina went straight to him, pecked him and said "thank you for making my day. Your presence is the best gift I have received in my entire life". It was like a dream for Mka, but he managed to thank Amina back and wished her better days ahead. This catalyzed Amina the more as she became more libidinous. Mka's voice was so masculine, deep and so calm for Amina's liking. She then asked Mka to follow her to her room. Without any word, Mka followed her like a sheep being dragged to slaughter. She held and dragged his left hand as they moved. It was a hotel room Amina had just paid for immediately she finished dancing with Mka. She wanted to appreciate him for dancing with her.

Mka was helplessly on the purple dressed bed as Amina pushed him and started kissing him so deeply. She unbuttoned his T shirt, kissed his black nipples, removed his trousers, and kissed his vein. Mka seemed to be lost as he did not know when Amina removed her dresses down to her bra. Mka who was initially "dead" was reactivated at the sight of what were perching on Amina's naked body. Her physique rang a bell that triggered Mka's pituitary gland. It was as though his testosterone had done an over secretion that night that sent an electronic signal to the deepest and most distant of Mka's tissues. On getting this signal, his innocent vein became as alert as an anaconda that was about to grab its prey. Its' elasticity was at its climax as it prayed for Amina to approach hither. As though she wanted him to salivate for more before she would pilot her cubicles closer to him, Amina stood some inches away, and was demonstrating her girlish gestures. Mka was speechlessly waiting earnestly for her to finish the enticement and walk close to the bed. He could not wait for her any longer. He grabbed and showed her the power of David over Goliath. When Amina finally walked towards him to the bed, the thought of his covenant with his God grabbed and made him impotent as his urge started dwindling. When Amina finally went for the "business" of the day to commence, Mka has gotten his moral sense completely, "wait wait wait, what is happening to us? Why are we here? Please I am not ready for that. Is this what I would get for dancing with you? Please I am sorry, I cannot do this. You know that we are not married and besides, we are meeting for the first time. I don't think I am in for this game now" Mka said. Amina who was already "soaked" managed to control her emotions. Tears started gushing down her eyes. "I am very sorry dear. I don't mean to embarrass you for dancing with me. It is true that you may be seeing me for the first time, but this is not the first I am seeing you. The first time I saw you was in the market, and since then, you have been part of me. I can't help how I feel about you. The greatest gift God gave me today as birthday gift was your presence. And you really made me happy by dancing with me. I want to pay you back. But I don't have any other thing to give you but what many boys had wanted from me. That is my virginity. Mka please be the first to 'dig me', I love you that much and I want to be your girlfriend". These words melted Mka. He was confused as he has not seen himself in that kind of temptation before apart from some years ago when he had an encounter with Linda in the snail hunting night. He paused helplessly as the room was calm for some seconds. Both of them were guessing at each other without uttering a fig. "See Amina, I so much appreciate how you feel about me. And I count myself privileged to have a beautiful angel like you offering me love. But I am sorry to tell you that I am still intact. And I don't know how to do it. Besides, it is true that a day begins a story, but for me, today is not the right day for the story to begin. It can begin sometime in future, not today. More so, I want to tell you that I have never been in love before, but today, I am beginning to feel love for you. So we can be friends, we can keep ourselves till when the right time comes".

Amina was very much satisfied with Mka. She never though he could speak such a good English with high sense of moral understanding. She was also ashamed of herself to have been blindfolded by infatuations. As the only daughter of a Muslim cleric, she was not supposed to be that cheap to a man. But even at that, she was still happy that at nineteen, she was a virgin which was very rare in Lagos. This is so because it was alleged that it would be easier for a blind man to see a pin than a virgin to be seen in Lagos. She was also happy that her infatuation has landed her to Mka. After some minutes of their discussion, Mka was the first to leave the room. Tolu was very happy when he saw him. To him, Mka has finally "dug" a girl. He went straight, shook Mka and off they went.

Amina's adventure with Mka saved him from Tolu's plans that night. He had planned to rent a room in the hotel after the party where he would drug him, while handing him over to a whore who would wake his vein with Viagra and sex him. But with Amina spending some minutes in a hotel room with Mka, he never discussed any such thing with Mka again as he had already concluded.

November, 2009 was coming to an end; Mka decided to go back to the village. Life in Lagos has never been fun for him. The only good thing he had in Lagos was Amina. Since after her birthday, Amina and Mka have become best of friends. Amina hardly stayed for a day without going to Boundary Market to see Mka. Although she would always claim that she was going to her father's shop. Nobody knew that Mka and Amina were best of friends except Tolu. Of course, Amina would not dare to tell her father that she was having an affair with an Igbo dude who happened to be a Christian too. It would be anathema before her father. Mka on his own has no need to tell Mr. Peter: after all, Amina was nothing but a mere friend to him.

On Tuesday, 1st December, 2009, Amina visited Mr. Peter's shop. She had earlier realized that something was bothering Mka. She sat close to Mka without any of them saying a word to the other. After about some minutes, she asked Mka on a very low tone what the problem was. Mka was surprised to hear such from her. He told her that all was well. When Tolu felt the two lovers could not discuss comfortably, he had to embark on exilic banishment. But still, Mka could not open up to Amina before her father Alhaji Mustafa called her for an errand.

It was indeed a lost opportunity for the two lovers to have good time together. On 15th of December, Mka opened up to Tolu by informing him that he was no longer at ease staying in Lagos. Business he said was not his calling. He wanted to go to the university. Tolu was not happy with the news because Mka's departure would cause him a lot of discomfort. He has for the past few months lived to believe that an Igbo boy could be best of friends unlike his previously held views. Personally, he had earlier realized that though Mka was coping with the business, he was never satisfied with it. But in as much as he considered his comfort with being with Mka, he was not selfish to neglect the comfort of the poor Igbo boy who wanted to become a graduate. To him, he has seen his lane. Gone were the days it was held that business was for the Igboman, while education was synonymous to the westerner. Such ethnic division of labour, as he has seen in Mka and himself no longer hold sway.

After some minutes of his mental discussion, Tolu asked Mka when he planned to leave. Mka could not give him any definite date because he had no money for his fare. Tolu further asked him if he has told their boss. Mka said no. "It dey good as you never tell am. If you tell am, he no go allow you. Me we suck the same breast with am never even get transport money to go home since ten years wey I don dey stay with am for Lagos. If I tell am say I wan go village em go say make I trek go naa. Em no get money for my transportation" Tolu further asked him if Amina was aware of his plan to travel, He replied no. Tolu, therefore, advised him to tell Amina about his intention. Tolu's advice for Mka not to inform his own senior brother while informing Amina was based on his findings. Through his contact with Amina and Mka, he has concluded that ethnicity was just a negative concept that rids people of their communion with their "distant brothers". He has as well come to believe the hard truth: the truth that the vastness of Nigeria and different ethnic groups are advantages and varieties that must be extracted and appreciated. He has seen genuine and spotless love between Mka and Amina. He has believed that love is good if it has elements of culture and mutual understanding. Finally, Tolu further promised Mka that he would do everything within his reach to raise transport fare for him. This assurance changed Mka's mood. He became very happy as he knew he would soon go home.

Although he has no clue of what fate had for him in the village, he would nevertheless want to go home. Tolu and Mka finally fixed December 24th for Mka's travel. They also agreed that Mr. Peter would be told on the 20th.

Although Amina would neither be happy nor support the plans, he Mka, did not want to take her unawares as that could hurt her. After morning market that day, Mka went to Alhaji's shop, greeted him and engaged him in some minutes of discussion. Alhaji was indeed delighted to hear the grammatical conduct of the poor "Igbo boy" as he would always call him.

Alhaji: You speak good English Mka, why did you not continue your education…? Oh! You like egusi business.

Mka: I have not said I like it sir; though I am into it already.

Alhaji: But that was what you came from the East to do. Any way, how old are you?

Mka: I am 20 years old, Sir.

Alhaji: Just a year older than my only daughter, Amina. But she is doing her Pre-degree at the Amadu Bello University, Zaria. It could have been better if you are in the university by now because you are very intelligent.

Mka: Thank you very much, Sir. I would have been in the University as you said, but my parents are not financially buoyant enough to send me to the University. Sir, you said that your daughter is in the university already: what is she studying?

Alhaji: That is one major problem we have in this country. Everything is very expensive and in a monetized world as ours, wisdom perishes in the mind of the less privileged who lack the resource to push ahead. He (the poor) has the wisdom, but lacks the medium of expressing and contributing it to the society. May Allah help us out of this mess. As for my daughter you asked after, she is doing her pre-degree in Sociology and Anthropology.

Mka: She is very lucky to have a father who can send her to the university not minding that she is a girl. Sir I have to commend you for that because I heard that Muslim Hausas hardly send their daughters to school. Amina must be very proud to have you as her father.

Alhaji: If I can't give my daughter the right and best exposure she deserves who else can give her that. She has to be educated so that she will stand the test of time. And besides, for a man to think of marrying her, he must acknowledge the fact that Amina is not like every other lady who does not know her left form her right.

Mka: That is true sir. But I wish I can see her so that

I will make some inquiries from her about JAMB and other related issues because I am thinking of taking the bull by the horn by next year.

Alhaji: Oh! That could have been okay but she travelled back to the North yesterday with my brother that visited. Though she said she did not want to travel then because she would miss her friends, but I gave her no option.

Mka: (*very angry; knowing fully well that he was the friend that the girl has protested that she would miss*) Ok sir. I have to join my brother in our shop now. Thanks for your advice.

Mka left for their shop entirely dejected. How could this Hausa man force that innocent girl home so suddenly, he pondered. He broke the news to Tolu who was as well sorry about the development. But there was nothing they could do. Tolu promised him that he would look for a way to get a contact through which Amina and Mka would communicate again. They left very early that day to prepare dinner because since 15th, people have started travelling to their villages. As such, after morning market, one could hardly sell in the evening. After dinner that evening, Mka told their boss his intention to travel on the 24th. But Mr. Peter pretended as though he was deaf. It was after some minutes that he asked Mka if he really knew what he was talking about. "How possible do you think it is for you to travel without telling me since November" he asked. "Anyway you are not doing anything for me here so if you have your moto money, bye bye" he concluded.

To him, he has dismissed the idea of travelling by indirectly informing Mka that he has no money to give him for transportation not to talk of money to buy other things he would need to travel with. But it surprised him on 23$^{rd}$ morning when Mka reminded him that he was still travelling the following day. Mr. Peter pondered on how and where Mka may have gotten transport fare. The boys had given account of their sales for the past three weeks and everything was accurate. He did not respond to Mka's notification. Even Mka was not sure of himself. He had no money to travel. It was only Tolu's assurance that he had; but he had kept all his belongings tidy for the travel which Tolu's magnanimous pocket would finally decide.

On their way to the shop that morning, Mka asked Tolu how possible it was for him to make it by the following day. He was assured as usual that the journey would be carried out. After morning market that day, Tolu left and never to return till after three hours. He came back with a medium sized Ghana Must Go Bag filled with new clothes and a pair of shoe. He told Mka that it was his luggage though he would have to leave their house with his old bag so that Mr. Peter would not be suspicious. When they closed for the day, the boys took Mka's new bag to Peace Mass Transport Company's park where they paid for Mka's ticket for the second bus that would leave on the 24<sup>th</sup>. The plan was that they would tell Mr. Peter that Mka would join a free transport that the government of Imo State has provided. The bus, they would tell Mr. Peter would leave on 24<sup>th</sup> night but Mka had to leave very early in the morning in order to catch up with the it. Getting home that day, they discovered that Mr. Peter who was suspicious of his boys' plans had ransacked the whole room looking for both new clothes and money. He had thought that Tolu may have connived with Mka to squeeze out money for his journey. He had to search their bags, and possibly bring out the money wherever they were hiding it to show them that he was the chairman of the house. But after a thorough searching, he could not see anything that showed that Mka was travelling. The only sign of that was that he has washed and arranged his clothes in his old Ghana Must Go bag. Mr. Peter who was still skeptical of what was happening asked Mka the means of his travelling. It was then that he told him that he would follow a free bus sent by the Imo State government. That lessen the suspicion to an extent.

Very early on 24<sup>th</sup>, the boys had dressed up. Mka was to be heading to the East while Tolu would be going to the shop. Mr. Peter barely bade Mka good bye because it was not in his interest to let the boy go. They went straight to the shop, Tolu brought out his apron and gave Mka Ten Thousand Five Hundred Naira. This got Mka dumbfounded. He never in life thought that a friend from another ethnic group could help him that much. Ten thousand Naira was indeed a very huge sum. He thanked him so heartily and left.

Mka was warmly welcomed by the parents, though it took them by surprise to have their son back from Lagos. The initial plan was that Mka would stay for at least two years before he could come home. Odu pondered on what could make his son return sooner than planned. He concluded that there must be something wrong somewhere. But on a second thought, he trusted his son. But what could cause his "sudden deportation?" He kept asking himself. Obiageri was very happy. For the first time a fruit of his womb would come back from the city during Christmas period. He may have not bought any piece of wrapper for her, but there was still hope for the future. Mka's siblings were all happy. Their senior brother had returned from Lagos. That implies that other children from the neighborhood would come to have a share of Cabin Biscuit from them. It indeed gave them a sense of belonging. Thanks to whatever circumstance that may have caused Mka's return. The Christmas celebration was indeed well spent with full happiness in Odu's family. Both Isinna and Ezeji who have been living with Aunty Rebecca all came back too.

As for Mka, three things kidnapped his happiness. The thought of how to start the next year and how he would go through the year. To him, he needed to be in the university as soon as possible. But his SSCE result was not yet out. It was only the NECO result that was out and he did not make Literature in English which he must pass in order to study his dream course, law. So over his education, he has two issues to tackle: His O level result and JAMB. The second thing that took Mka's happiness was that he was missing his newly and first ever female friend: Amina. He had not been in love before. But this time around, nature and other forces have denied him access to the lady she has seen as special in his life. He was engulfed with the thought of when and how to meet Amina again. The third puzzle was how to pay Tolu for his gestures and care towards him. To him, it is rare for "Ndi Ofe-Mmanu" to be kind to an Igbo person. But Tolu has given him another perception of the Yorubas'. He believed that having "robbed" his blood brother to please him, he owe Tolu a whole lot. He, therefore, had it as a burden to see Tolu again and possibly reciprocate his kindness.

It was 31$^{st}$ December, and Mka knew that he would be going to the church for "Cross Over" night. Gathering in the church for thanksgiving and dedication has been a routine every last day of the year. Mka has learnt to write down his achievements on every 31$^{st}$ December in order to evaluate himself. At that night, as usual, he prayed fervently for God to lead him through 2010.

After the new year service, Mka visited his long time mentor. Bro Mathew. He was then a priest in the Anglican Church, married with three kids. Rev Mathew was surprised to see Mka because they lost touch since Mka left Bro Godwin's house. Mka has been avoiding him because Rev. Mathew has told him that the former was called by God to be an ordained priest. On his own, that was contrary to what Mka has known about himself. He has been counselled during his days in the seminary not to give heed to people's suggestions over his future. The students' counsellor would always tell them that there were two people that could determine one's future: God and the person involved. He advised that before they make choices of future careers, they have to fast and pray fervently for God to direct them on what to do. She further added that whatever God would say must be in line with the skills he has put on the individual right from birth. According to her, any prophecy, advice, move that is contrary to this, is a deception that one must regret at the end of the day. Mka had to fast and pray after his JSCE exam. Telling God to reveal to him what His plans for him were. He fasted and prayed for 14 days before the session resumes for him to be in the Senior Secondary School. His target was to be sure of God's plans for him so that he would know whether he would join either the Science or Art classes. On numerous occasions, he dreamt of himself being a lawyer; though not a practicing lawyer. So he concluded that he would study law in the University of Nigeria, Nsukka and after his studies, would be a politician. Juxtaposing his personal dreams, skills and what he thought was God's revelations to him in dreams, he concluded that he would study law but would not be practicing. But how else could God expose Himself to the poor boy who knows little about other disciplines studied in the University? Based on his level of exposure, there were two things one could study in the tertiary institution: Arts and Science. While studying science would land one in the hospital as a doctor or nurse, studying law would land one in the court as a lawyer or politics. To him, there is no other discipline studied in the university. As such, Mka deserved no blame when he held that he would study law to become a politician. On the same hand, God is such wise that he ministers to one based on their levels of understanding. With all these, Mka was madly in love with his chosen career and the chosen University. He loved this the way a man could love a woman. And in order to achieve this aim irrespective of his poor family background, he had made the Biblical Joseph, Esther and Daniel his models. He liked Joseph and Esther because Aunty Ocha has told them during Sunday School that the two biblical youths were able to get to the apex of the societal ladder because they reserved their virginity for God. Daniel on his own side made fame because, among other things, he refused eating things that could spoil one, alcohol. So Mka decided to live like these three biblical youths. As a matter of fact, anyone that tells Mka anything contrary to this view is nothing but an enemy to his progress.

In the light of this, Mka lost interest in visiting

Rev. Mathew who would always tell him how he would be ordained a priest. When Mka got to the Reverend's house that day, he was warmly welcomed by the man of God who started calling him "The Runaway Jonah". After lunch, Mka told the Reverend how confused he was about life. He did not know where to start the year from. After explaining everything, the Reverend asked him about his SSCE result and Mka told him that Literature in English has been a barrier for him. The Reverend boasted that it was God that seized the result because without it, Mka would not study Law. He further told him, it was a way of God telling Mka that he was to be a priest. He then informed the confused lad that the Diocese was accepting applications for employment of Evangelists. He assured Mka that he would buy form for him to be employed as an Evangelist in the church. He prophetically told Mka that if he accepts the offer, his result would be released before March that year. And that the literature result would be very good, but Mka would not use it again as he would be a priest. Mka who was not willing to wear the cassock had to accept the offer. His acceptance was not because he has been convinced. He believed that his result would be released as he has prayed fervently over it reminding God that he has been keeping the covenant of virginity he had with him. He challenged God to fulfill His own part of the covenant. Furthermore, he has accepted being an evangelist to fulfill the plan he had in Lagos the previous year: delving into anything that would yield him money for him to go to the university. As soon as they have agreed, the Reverend wrote an application letter and gave it to Mka to recopy in his own handwriting. After that, he gave Mka transport fare to take the letter to the Diocesan Clerical Synod Secretary: Rev. Edet Obichukwu who was living in the Bishop's court.

On Thursday, 14th January, 2010, the applicants were invited for interview. A total number of Thirty applicants went for the interview; Mka was the last to be invited because his application letter was the last to be received. By the time he went in, most of the interviewers were famished already. It was only his name that he was asked for and was told to go.

The interview had ended and Mka was on his way home when he saw one of his schoolmates Chibuike Onuegbu who informed him that their results were released. Mka's feeling over this was a mixed one. He was happy that his result was released, but does it mean that he would be an ordained priest as Rev. Mathew prophesied earlier? He managed to thank Chibuike for the information as they parted. The following day, he went to his alma mater to see the result. The school has resumed the previous week. The result he saw complicated everything. Rev. Mathew prophesied a nice result. Mka was expecting a nice result too. But it baffled him to see that the literature was F9. For one thing, having F9 to him proved that Rev. Mathew's test to God has been defeated. After all, the Reverend prophesied a nice result. But on the other hand, he was sad. How could he make an F9 result? It means that his plan to buy JAMB form that year has been defeated. In the face of this mixed feelings, life still had to go on for the poor boy.

By Tuesday, 19th the result of the screening exam was out. Mka has been selected and employed as an Evangelist. The orientation course was slated to start by Monday 25th January and lasts through Friday morning.

## CHAPTER FIVE

# THE EVANGELIST

**THE ORIENTATION** course ended with everyone obtaining their posting letters. The Diocesan Laity Director: Rev. Can. Chym Ukolie and his team of invited guests really took their time to equip the employees. They were taught Anglicanism, what it means to be a pastor in the 21$^{st}$ Century, how to tackle the problems of the congregation and so on. The first place Mka went was to the house of Rev. Mathew. He showed him his posting letter indicating that Mka had to work under a superior priest in the same church. There were still others who were posted to churches where they would be the only workers. After there, Mka immediately went to Umuagba to inform his people of his posting. He was welcomed with great joy by everyone. It was indeed seen as a privilege to have an evangelist in the family. Someone who would always be alert in the spirit to wage wars against evil spirits that would try to trouble the family. That night, the only thing that left undone was for Mka to be worshipped. As early as 7am the following day, people gathered in Odu's family. The news of Evangelist Mka had spread itself far and near. People have started coming to have prayers from the young flaming Evangelist.

At around 12noon when visitors reduced, Mka had to go to his home church to see the resident Catechist. It was an old man. Catechist Adiego was in his early seventies and was no longer strong for his pastoral works. After some time with him, Mka informed him that he would be packing to his place of assignment by Monday evening. The catechist promised him that the church would raise fund for him during the worship the following day which was Sunday. This gladdened Mka's heart because he was not sure of how he could get money for his journey and to buy some necessary things he needed.

On the Sunday evening, Mka visited the catechist. The church has done freewill donation during the service. That evening, Mka did not see the catechist. He was told to come back later as the man of God was having some rest. Mka returned in the following two hours, but the catechist had gone out and would not be back till around 8pm in the night. Mka was disorganized. He had planned to go to Rev. Mathew's house that evening from where he would pack to his place of assignment the following day. After some minutes in the parsonage, he went home. He took some food stuffs his mother had prepared for him and left for Rev. Mathew's house.

The Rev. was not happy when he heard that Mka could not get any support from his home church. That was not a surprise to him. He has been in the system. That night, Mka and Rev Mathew could not sleep on time. The Rev. took his time to tell Mka all he thought he needed to know. He advised him not to rub shoulders with his boss, to be careful with church girls, money and to take his prayers very serious. After the advice, he gave Mka two cassocks, a black and a white one with one white supplest. Although the cassocks could contain three Mkas at a time, but the lad was very happy with the Rev.'s care. After their time together, Mka went to the church. He decided that he would not sleep that night. He wanted to sort everything out personally with his God. After some minutes of worship songs that night, he brought out the paper where he has documented what he termed his agreement with God. In the agreement he wrote on the 31st December 2009, he has itemized so many things he wanted God to do for him that year. Among them was to have his literature result released, gain admission into the university, and so on. He as well wrote that he would keep his virginity throughout the year in as much as God would grant his heart desires.

But on that night, he thought the agreement needed an amendment because it was obvious that he would not make it to the university that year; his O Level result was not complete. As such, he needed to add and remove some things from the agreement. So the amendment read thus

AN AGREEMENT MADE BETWEEN THE MOST HIGH AND I: MKA ON DECEMBER, 31ST, 2009 AS AMENDED ON THIS 31ST JANUARY, 2010

Dear lord, thank you for thus far you have lead me. Because of your faithfulness and concern towards my welfare, I promise you the following this year

- I will keep my flower for you till my wedding night.
- I will pray at least ten minutes every day.
- I will fast a least twice a week
- I will make sure that I live in peace with everyone.
- I will make sure that I will be a good evangelist.
- I will not steal from church treasury, nor have any affair with my church girls.
  These are some of the things I want you to do for me this year
- I want you to grant me the grace to fulfil my own part of our agreement.

- I want you to use this period I will be serving as an evangelist to clarify me on what you want my future to be like.
- I want you to help me maintain by love and zeal for education.
- I want you to provide an avenue through which I would meet Amina and Tolu again.
- I want you to bless my family, the family of Rev. Mathew and all my well-wishers.
- I want you to give me grace before my boss.

I am sealing this agreement with my virginity and the blood of Jesus.

After reading the agreement like someone making incantations, Mka who was lying before the altar busted into tears.

By the following morning, things were made ready for him to go to his station. Mrs. Petra Mathew had brought out many things to support Mka. At around 3:30 pm, two motorcyclists were hired to take him to St. Silas Anglican Church Rowa. One of the motorcycles would carry all his properties while the other one would carry Mka, Ijeoma, and Chibuzo. Ijeoma and Chibuzo were Rev. Mathew's cousins who were living with him. On getting to the church compound, some youths were waiting for their new pastor to arrive. Mka has already entered the Evangelists' house, prayed, arranged his properties and went to his boss house to sign in. The youths were still waiting.

It was getting dark already, Ijeoma and Chibuzo had left, the youths have waited and gone without seeing what they were looking for, Mka had signed in in the office of his boss and came back to his lonely apartment. That night, he hardly prayed, he was thinking of how and where to start as evangelist.

The following morning, after his morning devotion, Mka went to his boss, Ven. Ehiem's house. Ven. Ehiem was a true Born Again Christian. He was already blessed with four sons. He informed Mka that there would be PCC meeting in the evening. One of the agenda was to introduce him to the PCC. He also gave Mka some church documents that he said would be under his custody. After that, Mka left to prepare for the meeting. At about 4:15pm, the PCC were fully seated for the meeting. The Ven. said the opening prayers and few words of admonition. The next thing was the introduction of the new evangelist. The PCC were not happy when they knew that the new evangelist was a bachelor. Like the youths, they wanted a married man. But nobody could question the authority that posted Mka to their church. They welcomed him though with mixed feelings. After the meeting that day, the Ven. called Mka and beseeched him to be very careful with everything in the church.

Few weeks have passed, and Mka was getting used to the whole environment. The congregation as well was getting to know him better. They have as well started liking him because he was giving his best in the Children's Ministry. For instance, within the first one month of Mka's presence in St Silas, the children could recite the sixty-six books of the bible offhand. They have as well-known many bible stories and characters. Their lives were beginning to change too. These fetched Mka the love of the parents of the children. But even at that, no parent would want their female children no matter the age to stay in the church compound beyond 6pm. This was because of Evangelist Chinedu that Mka replaced. He had a terrible character.

One Monday evening, Mka could not dismiss the children by 6pm. Before long, mothers were trooping into the church premises to take home their children. To Mka, this was very embarrassing and disrespectful, but he could not restrain them. He then had to officially dismiss the children. Later that evening, Madam Agnes, one of the women who had developed trust in Mka went to the Evangelists' apartment. She had earlier taken home her children; but her mind was blaming her for doing that without Mka's permission. When she got to the church, Mka was sitting outside his apartment reading his bible. After they greeted, she told him how sorry she was for behaving the way she did some hours back. She told him that the villagers were no longer at ease with Evangelists especially the single ones. This she said started for a very long time; but the immediate past

Evangelist aggravated matters. Chinedu was involved in incessant sexual immorality with the church girls irrespective of age. He got three girls pregnant within a year. He was also a notorious thief. The whole thing was surprising to Mka. To him, a church worker was not expected to think of any sinful act not to talk of engaging in it.

Mka and his boss have been living peacefully for the past five months. But between him and the Venerable's wife, there was a Cold War. Violence has not broken out because, among other things, Mka was not yet married. Severally, Mka has heard that the wives of priests are always the causes of problems in the parsonage, but being into the system, he has seen things for himself. St Silas had a very large church compound. Even outside the church premises, there was a very massive land that belonged to the church which was filled with lots of palm and other economic trees. Conventionally, workers in the church cultivated the land. The senior worker who happened to be the venerable was to share the land and the economic trees. That was how the church committee made it to be. But contrary to that, the Venerable's wife accumulated everything for herself alone. He saw Mka as a minor Evangelist who should not have a portion in the church's properties. On his own part, Mka was not interested in Church properties. To him, being in the parsonage was highly transitory for him. All he needed was to raise money, write JAMB, gain admission into the university and go his way. As such, all the maltreatments mounted on him by the Venerable's wife were seen as not worth distracting him.

But one day, Mka decided to speak out. The church members had told him to cultivate a small land adjacent to his house. They said that was where other evangelists used as their garden. The Venerable had told Mka that that portion belonged to him. He mandated Mka to plant vegetable there because he must bring something for church harvest thanksgiving. Mka had done the work with the help of the church youths. As though the God of farming was with him alone, his plants did very well and got matured within a short period of time.

One day, Mka had gone for Laity school. It was monthly gathering of all the evangelists and catechists within the diocese. That day, when Mka got home, he discovered that his garden had been grazed. He was surprised as to who could have done that. He was not suspecting anybody because he believed that nobody in their right senses could do that. Mka immediately went to the Venerable's house to tell him what had happened. But the venerable could not utter anything upon hearing Mka's story. He did not want to enter into another quarrel with the wife who was the culprit. Before Mka came back from the laity school, the venerable and the wife had quarrels over the issue. As Mka was leaving through the Venerable's backdoor, he saw his farm proceeds where they were heaped. It was then he knew that the mistress was the culprit. He also understood why the Venerable could not utter any word regarding his complaint.

That day, Mka spent the whole night very angry. He wanted to take the bull by the horn by confronting his mistress, but the thought of the Venerable calmed him down. This attitude of the Venerable's wife made him to hate pastoral work the more. His whole prayers were for things to work out well for him so that he could leave for his university education.

The following month, Mka attended laity school. That month's own was a couples' school. The married catechists and evangelists were meant to attend with their wives. The essence of this was for the workers' wives to be groomed alongside their husbands, so that together, they could do the missionary work better. To Mka's greatest surprise, the female lecturer for the day was Mrs. Ngozi Ehiem, the wife of the venerable. Mrs. Ehiem was to deliver a lecture on the topic, "The Conduct of the Workers' Wives in her Local Churches". During the lecture, the woman explained everything a good worker's wife was expected to do. She urged them to be caring to neighbors, live exemplary lifestyle before the congregation, and so on. It was indeed a well prepared lecture. After the lecture, she urged all the women to step out to the altar. Mrs. Ngozi commanded the power of the Holy Spirit that day such that almost all the women were crying as they were falling under the anointing. The woman of God prophesied and laid curses on anyone that would resort to sin after that day. That day, to everyone except Mka and Evangelist Chinedu, Mrs. Ngozi was the most spirit-filled priest's wife in the whole diocese. Mka was very surprised and disappointed that God could allow His Holy Spirit to attend to Mrs. Ngozi's prayers. A woman that had never gave her husband peace at home. Even the whole congregation in St Silas knew that Mrs. Ngozi was nothing to write home about. How could God allow her to pray and people would fall under the anointing? From that day, Mka became skeptical of people falling under the anointing.

After the school, the workers happily moved to the Church dining hall. It was a routine for them to have lunch at the end of each school. Mka was the only one not smiling as they were seating for meal. He was not comfortable with God, Holy Spirit and his Mistress. But there was nothing he could do. As the lunch was going on, people were discussing in cliques. The major topic was how powerful and spirit-filled Mrs. Ngozi Ehiem was. Most workers were saying that they would like to be posted to the same church with the woman; others were saying other manners of good things about her. Evangelist Chinedu in his own clique was poke nosing those admiring Mrs. Ngozi. To him, they were admiring her because they have not gotten close to her. He was telling his clique how Mrs. Ngozi maltreated him the time they were serving in the same church. He remembered how he has leant to eat "church's pawpaw" from Mrs. Ngozi. Mrs Ngozi would always invite him when the Venerable was aware and would display some amorous behaviour before him. But he would always rebuff the woman's gestures. One day, Mrs. Ngozi set a trap for him. She had invited Amarachi one of the most beautiful and sexy girls in the whole parish and gave her some money in order to lure Evangelist Chinedu to bed.

That night, the Venerable was not in town. He attended Church of Nigeria Clergy conference at Ibadan. It was drizzling when at about 7:30pm, there was a knock on the evangelist's door. As he opened the door, it was Amarachi. She claimed that she was going for Parish Girls Guild's night vigil before it started drizzling. She pleaded with the evangelist to allow her to wait in his house for the rain to stop for her to continue her journey to the Extension Church where the vigil was to take place. Evangelist Chinedu with a clear heart allowed her in. Soon, it began to rain so heavily. The two were chatting in the evangelist's sitting room. They have exhausted all that could be discussed. But it was still raining. "Sir why are you still single; you supposed to have married" Amarachi said. Chinedu replied that the Holy Spirit had not yet directed him to do that. "Hmm. He has to ooo. A handsome evangelist like you will have many admirers, so the Holy Spirit should speak before girls would lead you into temptation". But Chinedu opposed falling into temptation. "Do you mean that if I make myself available for you to do anything you want you will not accept me?" She asked. But Chinedu could not say anything in answer. He immediately changed the topic. But even at that, Amarachi has sent a signal that was rumbling in his mind throughout that night. By the time it stopped raining, it was already 11:45 Pm. Amarachi pleaded to spend the night as it was late for her to continue her journey. He accepted the request and told her that she would sleep in the bedroom while he sleeps in the sitting room. Some minutes after they have gone to bed, Amarachi tiptoed nakedly into the sitting room. It was dark. Chinedu had left his only lantern for her in the bedroom. Although he noticed that she entered the sitting room, he could not say anything. He thought that the lady wanted to go to the bathroom to ease herself. Chinedu was battling on the question he was asked some minutes back. Skillfully, she kicked her leg against the cushion where Chinedu was lying and fell on him. As he tried to make a move, the first place he touched was her succulent breast. He became surprised that she was naked. Before he could utter a word, Amarachi was already kissing and caressing his sex-starved vein. Immediately, the evangelist took charge of the whole game. They had foreplay for some minutes. As there was no light in the sitting room, the two had it as rough as their strength could carry them. When they were done, Amarachi pleaded for both of them to sleep in the bedroom. There was no longer reason why Chinedu could refuse that. He has eaten what he was previously avoiding to see not to talk of touching. "I for say oooo, I wanted to know if I am that ugly that you would refuse me. Did you not enjoy me this night?" Amarachi playfully asked. "So you daughter of Jezebel came to seduce a handsome and innocent pastor like me right? By the way, how on earth do you think a right thinking man would withstand your beauty? Amara you have really showed me what God saw in you daughters of Eve that made Him say he who finds you finds a good thing. You are indeed super sweet" said Evangelist Chinedu as they continued the after sex chat. The way Chinedu handled her that night made her fall deeply in love with him. She decided not to continue with the initial arrangement she had with the Venerable's wife. She knew that what Mrs. Ngozi wanted was to have a taste of Chinedu. That was not the first she used her to have access to men she needed. As for Chinedu's case, okwala ya. She decided that she would protect him so dearly that no other woman would see the color of his 'holy' sperm.

As early as 5:30am, Amarachi left. Like other girls coming back from the night vigil, she was looking tired but no one knew exactly what made her look the way she was looking. In the afternoon, she got a message telling her that the Venerable's wife was calling her. She knew what the call was for.

When Amarachi got to the parsonage, she was asked why she did not play the game she was paid for. She lied that the rain could not allow her to come out not to talk of going to the evangelist's apartment. The Venerable's wife gave her a second chance to perform, but she outrightly told her that she could not continue with the deal. When she was asked to bring back the money she was paid, she threatened to expose her. From that moment, their deal ended. One day, after a hot afternoon sex with Chinedu, Amarachi confessed the circumstance that brought both of them together. But even at that, Chinedu who was blindly in love with her could not leave her.

After he remembered this, Chinedu told his clique that clergy wives are the source of a greater percentage of the evil performed by junior workers. As he was saying that, Mka joined them in their group. He wanted not to say anything, but he could not withhold himself. He narrated the story of how the Holy Mrs. Ngozi had been treating him. Before long, the lunch was over and everyone departed.

Mka got home that day very disappointed and famished. But it was not yet time to rest as the church had choir practice that evening. As Mka got to the church, there was no one there. He bent his head on one of the pews to have a nap as he waited for the choristers. Within some minutes, he discovered that Pastor Christian was waiting for him. Pastor Christian a renowned minister in Jesus the Saviour of the World Evangelical

Church. He has made name for himself by conducting family and community liberations. Pastor Christian was said to have raised a dead man after some hours of his death. His cases of healing, uprooting charms and other miraculous works were much. Mka was glad to have been visited by this renowned man of God. After offering him a bottle of coke and biscuit, the pastor thanked and invited him for a revival program in his church. But Mka refuse by telling him that he was not good in conducting deliverance so he should look for another person capable of letting people fall under the anointing. This was indeed a surprise to Pastor Christian. He expected something similar to that knowing full well that the Anglicans and the Roman Catholic Churches are not as radical as the New Generation Churches. To him, who in this ministry could not pray down people under anointing? How can such minister excel? He insisted that Mka should come to preach while another person would do the deliverance session. This was okay by Mka who admitted to go.

After the event that night, Pastor Christian thanked Evangelist Mka a lot for the wonderful message he gave. He asked Mka why he was not willing to have the grace to deliver people from the satanic bondages. When Mka replied that God has not given him such gift and that he was not desperate for it, Christian laughed at him deeply. He told him that without the grace to do deliverance, no pastor in the ministry would succeed. He further reminded him that the Bible says that since the days of John the Baptist, the kingdom of God suffers violence and the violent takes it by force. He told Mka that if God did not give him that gift, it was intentional by God to see how determined he was to get himself equipped for the work of God. He reminded him that Jesus Christ had to order that the man with one talent who felt that he was okay with that one talent should be rid of it. While the man with five talents was given more talents. He advised Mka to make a move towards getting the grace to liberate people from the satanic bondage. He told him how willing he was to help him get all the necessary things he needed for the ministry. After that, he gave Mka the sum of Twenty Thousand Naira. Mka was surprised to have made such a sum just by preaching. The pastor further told him that he initially planned to give him Fifty Thousand Naira when he thought that Mka could say both the message and conduct the deliverance session. But as another man of God did that, he had to share the money between them.

Mka went home that night happy. Just for a night's ministration, he was able to make Twenty Thousand Naira. An amount that was equivalent to his two months' stipend. That night, he prayed to God for extra oil. He reminded God of their covenant; God had no reason not to grant him his heart desire was his belief. After the prayers that night, he went to bed, he dreamt of a man on a white robe directing him to go to Pastor Christian for help. When he woke up, he could not understand the dream. But as he dreamt, he had to go to Jesus the Savior of the World Evangelical Church to see Pastor Christian. He narrated his dream to the pastor who told him that it was the Holy Spirit who had directed him on what to do. He asked Mka to come later in the day for them to pray together.

That evening, when Mka visited, Pastor Christian was said to be having his siesta. He waited patiently till around 6pm. When they finally met, the pastor told him how sorry he was for keeping him waiting. He asked Mka if he really needed the grace to do deliverance. Mka replied in agreement. He then told him that they would pray together that night. The prayer he said would be on a mountain where no one would distract them. Being desperate to be equipped for the work of God, Mka did not refuse a man who wanted to help him become a powerful evangelist. That night, they left Pastor Christian's house around 9pm. It took them three hours to get to a certain mountain. Mka was told that they would have to walk a bit farther before they could pray. As they walked some few minutes, Mka saw some men of God from different denominations coming from the opposite direction. He was surprised. He asked Pastor Christian where the people were coming from and he told him that they were coming from the same mountain they were going to. They have gone earlier and God has given them what they went for. That was why they were coming back en-mass. As they walked for few minutes, Mka started hearing some strange sounds. Before long, he saw a thatched house decorated with human skeleton and other strange objects. He was very afraid. To him, he has really known the source through which many men of God get their powers. As he tried to ask Pastor Christian a question, he got a tap on his back. It was the choirmaster who came for the choir practice. It was then that Mka realized that it was a dream. He has fallen asleep while waiting for the choristers to come before the choir could start

The dream was a very strange one for him. Does it mean that people obtain power to perform miracles from base spirits? He pondered. Although Mka could not completely believe his dream, he was uncomfortable being in the church the more. But how could he leave the church that soon? He has only succeeded in writing GCE exam and has cleared his papers apart from Mathematics. But he was not worried about Mathematics. He did the exam on his own without any external help. He planned to combine his GCE with his NECO result because he made an A in mathematics in NECO.

By December, 23rd, 2010, Mka registered for JAMB examination. By 31st night, he had made ready his agreement with God for the year 2011. His major request therein was to gain admission into the university. He decided to either study in the University of Nigeria, Nsukka or Ahmadu Bello University, Zaria. His choice of Ahmadu Bello was to see if he could meet Amina whom he has lost contact with. In order to make it to any of these universities on the merit list, Mka wrote in the agreement paper that he would fast and pray from January, 1st to any day the JAMB exam would be taken. He also decided to study very hard.

## CHAPTER SIX

# THE STUDENT

**MKA HAD** waited for the admission list of Ahmadu Bello University Zaria to be out. He made up his mind to study there. His recent choice of the ABU over the initial UNN was spurred by three major reasons. One, he wanted to live somewhere outside Igboland. Two, he wanted to live in a place dominated by another religious group other than Christianity. The third reason no matter how flimsy it may look was as strong as the other reasons, to see if he could seize the opportunity to meet Amina again.

To make his admission pursuit easy for him in a globalized world, Mka has bought a Nokia Symbian phone, created both yahoo mail and Facebook accounts. One day, as he was Facebooking, a thought came into him to search for Amina Mustafa. Mka immediately queued in the name, and Amina's profile was among those that appeared. Mka spent much time feeding himself with the damsel's uploaded pictures. After which, he sent her a friend request with some message to explain himself. Having seen Amina's pictures after a long period of time was so satisfying for him. Throughout that day, he was very joyous. He frequently logged in to check if his request has been accepted.

By October, Mka heard over the radio that ABU had released her merit admission list. He quickly checked his admission status on JAMB website, and there was no admission for him. This depressed him. He felt disappointed. To him, nothing could make him not to be admitted on the first list. Therefore, he concluded that what people were saying was true. It has been said that it was very hard for one to gain admission to study in any university other than the ones within his ethnic group. More so, the few that could study outside their ethnic based universities were those admitted on the primary list. The subsequent lists would be those who know and those that know who know the Vice-Chancellors and the said universities' staff. Mka who was an Igbo boy knew no student in the ABU not to talk of a staff. If he had known, he could have looked for admission in any university within the Southern part of Nigeria. Mka, therefore, regretted not writing Post UTME exams with the UNN.

The following day, Mka logged into the Facebook. He had a message and a notification. He firstly clicked to check what the notification was. To his greatest surprise, Amina had accepted his friend request. He quickly checked his inbox, it was Amina chatting him up. Mka has never been that happy since he became an evangelist. He replied to Amina's message and before few minutes, she was online and they started an intensive chatting. Amina expressed how she missed him and how she had wanted to commit suicide when she heard from Tolu that Mka had left for the East and never to come to Lagos again. The chat which was started at about 5pm could not be stopped till Mka's phone gave him three beeps and tripped off. The battery was flat. Mka checked the time, it was already 9pm. He had forgotten to go for Cell Prayer that the church had by 6pm. He was not all that worried about that. After all, that was the first time he could miss a church program. Besides, if he missed it because he was having a chat with Amina, that was never a problem. Amina worth every time he could give her.

Mka immediately went to the Venerable's house to apologize for missing the Cell Fellowship. He told the venerable that he was sick and never knew that the pharmacist put some sleep inducing pills to his tablet. The venerable who had not seen Mka missing any activity before believed him immediately. After that, Mka went straight to the Venerable's sitting room to charge his phone, but as soon as he plugged it, the generator went off. There was little petrol in the engine. So disappointed was Mka that he left with his phone. That night, he was very happy and emotionally sick. The joy of chatting with Amina made him forget that the university was no longer for him that year. Immediately after Friday morning Holy Communion mass, Mka left for Isinweke to look for where he could charge his phone. He really needed to continue his chat with Amina. Fortunately for him, as he got to Isinweke, there was power. He went into a barbing saloon owned by one of his church members and plugged in his phone. As soon as the battery charged one percent, Mka powered it and went straight to Facebook, as he had thought since last night, Amina had dropped him many messages. He was happy as he read them. After reading, he told her that it was his battery that disappointed him the previous night. He therefore booked a chat with her by 6pm. He believed that by that time, both of them would be free with the day's activities. Mka bought extra phone battery and got the two of them fully charged so that nothing would interrupt his chat that night.

At exactly 6pm, Mka logged in to Facebook. He discovered that Amina was already online. He signaled her and they started their chat. After asking how they spent their days, Amina asked Mka about his zeal for education. He narrated to her everything about his life since they parted and finally told her how ABU frustrated his effort. She was indeed sorry to hear that.

She told Mka that she got admission the previous year and she was currently in her Second year. It was indeed a good news for Mka. He liked to hear people's success stories. Amina asked him the course he wanted to study in the ABU, and he answered Law. He further told her that he had an average mark of 255. Amina then saw the reason he could not make it with the first list. The university cutoff point for law in the primary list was 260. She assured Mka that with such a high score, his name would definitely be out in the second list; but then, he may be admitted to study a course other than law. Mka was pleased to hear that. Amina has been so special to him; her words gave him a ray of hope. That night, they chatted so deep. They discussed so many things about their lives before they finally went to bed around 2am.

Mka has been given reasons to go back to his prayers. He had regained his lost hope. He kept asking God to surprise him. On Wednesday 16th November, 2011, he logged in to Facebook around 7:50pm. There was a message in his inbox. He knew it was Amina that had sent it; but the message was unknown to him. When he finally opened it, the message read

"Congratulations my darling

Right from the onset, I knew you are a genius

I am proud to have you

We have made it"

Mka could not exactly understand what they have made. But he was thinking he may have gotten admission. But if it were to be admission, why would she say "we have made it". Was the admission for the both of them? He replied "lol…pls dear don't put me in suspense. What's it that we made?" Amina told him to guess. He naughtily said "you are pregnant for me". Amina laughed and told him that he should not forget that she was a daughter of a Muslim cleric. That she would not even think of being in love with a Christian not to talk of marrying him. Mka knew that she was not serious because they were in love already and could even marry based on the level of love they have for each other. Amina then asked Mka "What if you gain admission to study Philosophy, what would you do? Mka replied that he would be very glad and would start packing to school. Amina then said "Now start preparing to come to ABU to meet your queen. I can't wait to see that your big head soon…you have been given admission"

It was indeed a mind blowing news for Mka. And getting the news of his admission from Amina was the best of it all. After their chat that night, Mka had to check his admission status on the JAMB website. He was admitted to study Philosophy. Mka quickly ran to the Venerable's house and broke his good news. The man of God was so delighted to hear the news. He knew that Mka deserved it. He was both intelligent and hardworking. The following Sunday, the Venerable broke the news to the church. Everyone was very happy with their loved evangelist. Within one year and some months Mka had been in St Silas, he has shown that all evangelists are not the same. There were still those that knew their onus in the lord's vineyard. Though he never worked because he was called. He worked because he really needed to justify his pay.

By the following Monday, Mka got a text message from the ABU admission Unit telling him that he had to pay acceptance fee of Twenty Thousand Naira within seven days of receiving the text message. That meant that Mka had to go to Zaria that week. But he did not have the cash to do that. He had planned to resume school by January. Knowing not what to do, he called Amina on phone and informed her of the message he got. He also told her that he would be coming to Kaduna that week to get the fee paid though he was not sure of the money then. The church has not paid him for three months. Amina offered to help him by making the payment while Mka put everything in place to come by January. It was indeed a good suggestion for Mka. His challenge was then how to raise the money and send it across to her through her bank account number. Mka had told her to send him her bank account details before the day could run out. He decided to look for where to borrow money to send Amina the following day. But before the day could be over, Amina sent Mka a picture of an acceptance fee receipt. She had made the payment with her own money without sending Mka her bank details. She had Mka's necessary information because the later had sent them to her to help him in checking his admission status. Mka was not only blessed with Amina. He did not know how to show his appreciation. With the payment of the acceptance fee, Mka had regularized his admission.

By Saturday, 17th December, 2011, the diocesan relocation list was out. Mka has been granted study leave. The list also read that all movements would be effective from Monday, January 6th, 2012; Mka's sent forth ceremony was slated to hold on Sunday, January 5th. The whole church was filled that day. Everyone was ready to contribute to Mka's movement to Kaduna. He served with all his strength, and as such, should be given a befitting sent forth party. His valedictory sermon was taken from the Gospel of Saint John 14: 18 where Jesus was advising his disciples before he left for heaven not to loose hope as he was leaving them for good. He said, like apostle Paul would say in his epistles to the Philippians 1:21 that staying with them in the church would be good, but leaving them would be better. He said that the need to leave them was in order for them to meet again, as without parting, they would not meet again.

After the sermon, people started shading tears. To make more pathetic of the atmosphere, the children ministry could not finish their heart-touching farewell anthem as all of them started shading tears. After the service that day, to the surprise of everyone, the total sum of Two Hundred and Fifty Thousand Naira cash was raised for Evangelist Mka. There were also lots of food stuffs and other household utensils such as pot, cutleries, and so on which he would need for his living on campus. Unlike Catechist Adiego, the Venerable handed him over the money and advised him to remain concentrated in the lord Jesus Christ as he moved to school.

It was Saturday, 11th January, 2012; Mka had made ready his luggage the previous days. He was to leave as early as possible on that Saturday morning. His father was led to the sitting room as Mka went to take his bath. Odu was then blind. He had a fatal accident the previous year that affected his sight. As soon as Mka got ready, the whole family rained prayers on him. Odu and Obiageri gave him all the pieces of advice he needed for his journey and he left with two Motorcycles that were arranged for the purpose. Before long, Mka had gotten to Onitsha from where the journey to the North started. It was indeed a very long journey, but it was never boring for the university boy. He had fully charged his two phone batteries for the journey. He was busy on WhatsApp chat with Amina who was desperate to see her friend after a long period of two years. As Mka's bus was leaving Lokoja, there was a very severe hold up. Nobody could explain what caused the hold up till each of the buses on the road got to a particular point. The point was where robbers have comfortably wedged the road. They took turn to rob the buses. There was no movement in either directions of the road for more than two hours. When it was the turn of Mka's bus, as usual, everyone was rid of their phones and cash. It was only food stuffs that were not touched. Mka lost his phone, the Two Hundred Thousand Naira the church had raised for him. It was indeed a black day as not even one policeman was anywhere to be found. It was said that the police could hardly stay on such highways. They always get themselves stock together in towns collecting the sum of fifty Naira from motorists.

The journey to Kaduna from the East was very long one. The robbery further delayed the journey. At exactly 1:15pm on Sunday, Mka was at the Ahmadu Bello University, Zaria. It was indeed a very beautiful institution. He had nowhere to stay. He had lost Amina's contact with his phone. He managed to go to a nearby business centre to send Amina a Facebook message. He was aware that Amina could not get the message till Wednesday because she had exhausted her data bundle as she told him during their chat the previous day. The WhatsApp chat was possible because she had to use her airtime for that.

Lost in the vast University, Mka was fortunate to see a notice posted on a wall close it him. It reads THE NIGERIAN FEDERATION OF CATHOLIC STUDENTS WELCOMES BOTH OLD AND NEW STUDENTS TO THE CAMPUS. CALL THIS NUMBER FOR ANY ASSISTANCE: 08022849096.

Mka immediately copied down the phone number, went straight to the same place he had sent Facebook message to Amina and paid them to dial the number. Fortunately, before few minutes, some executives of the NFCS arrived, took Mka to their secretariat. After having his shower and a hot meal of Ofada rice served with fried plantain. Mka was given a form to fill in his bio data. As soon as he woke up the following day, he was greeted by a sister who informed him that his water was ready for his bath. She pointed to the bathroom where Mka had a very hot shower. Before he was out from the bathroom, his dinner was served. Mka enjoyed his hot tea with fried egg and bread. After the meal, he had time with Bro Bode. Bro Bode was a final year student of Economics department. He was from Ogun State. His oratory and moral uprightness earned him the president of the fellowship uncontestedly. After hearing the sad story of how Mka was robbed, he was so sorry; he wished the fellowship was financially buoyant enough to take care of Mka. But in all, he assured him that the fellowship would take care of his need till when he would be established. Mka was very happy to hear this. He was also very surprised by the gestures and warm welcome the fellowship gave him. The surprise was much because everyone he was seeing in the secretariat was either a Fulani, an Igala, Hausa and other Northern ethnic groups. It was just a sister called sister Uyime whom he later discovered was from the Southern Nigeria. She was the sister who previously told him that his meal and bath water were ready. Apart from his experience with Tolu, and Amina in Lagos last two years, he could not believe that anyone other from the Igbo Ethnic group could show an Igboman such level of hospitality and love. He has also concluded to join the Catholic Church throughout his stay in school. That could be very a bad news to his parents and any other person from the East who would hear that Evangelist Mka of the Anglican Church was cheaply converted to a Roman Catholic. But to him, there was nothing wrong with that. He believed that God is one. God does not belong to any denomination or even religion. If God was to be an Anglican, he had seen many bad things in the Anglican Church. If God should be a Pentecostal, he has seen through his dream some time ago how some Pentecostal pastors get their powers. If God should be a Roman Catholic, he has been an Anglican from childhood, and he has been a moral person who had peace of the mind as the bible would say, as such, God can never be a Catholic alone. If God should be a Christian, he has known Amina who was a Muslim and has been virtuous and morally upright. So to Mka, God is one. He belonged to no religion, denomination, ethnic group, race et'al. He only exposes himself to people based on their levels of understanding, religion, and denomination and so on. And he belonged to all mankind irrespective of the colour and belief system.

Throughout that day, Mka stayed at the NFCS secretariat. The thought of Amina has never left him for a minute, but he had to control himself. After all, he was amidst brothers and sisters in the lord. He was also very convinced that Amina must be restless wherever she was. But he could not help it. There was no way he could reach her and he dare not go to the Muslim Students Fellowship to look for a girl. To him, that would be tantamount to suicide.

Similarly, Amina had waited throughout Sunday and Monday, there was no call from Mka, and his number has always been switched off. She has as well spent the whole Monday standing in front of Philosophy Department checking if she could see Mka, but all was a futile effort. She thought Mka may have decided to shun her. After all, she had heard stories of how the Igbo were so tricky, smart and ready at any moment to outsmart people. Could it be that Mka thought that she would ask him for the Twenty Thousand Naira she paid for his acceptance fee? But that would be too childish for Mka to think that way she thought. To her, she loved Mka so dearly, and she believed that Mka loved her too. Mka would not be playing any game on her. She thought for a while how she could see her lover whom she believed has traveled all the way from the East to the same university community with her. She therefore concluded to buy cardboard papers write something and paste everywhere around Philosophy Department.

By Tuesday, Mka finally found his ways to the Philosophy Department. It was around 8am. When he got to the department, the general office was not yet ready to start attending to students. He then had to go down to the quadrangle to wait till the office opened properly. The quadrangle was the best in the entire school. It was beautified with flowers and umbrella trees that could ventilate it very well. The idea was such that philosophy students could relax there and have feelings of nature that could lead them to deep thoughts. But because of how beautiful it was, the students have christened it the "The Philosophical Garden of Eden". As Mka was surveying his environment, he saw a poster with the write up: TEAM AMINA MUSTAFA WELCOMES ALL THE FRESHERS TO THE CAMPUS. WE LOVE AND WISH YOU A HAPPY ACADEMIC YEAR. CALL 08037591933 FOR MORE INFO. The name tickled Mka. He got closer and discovered that the phone number was Amina's. Though he did not have the entire number offhand, but he knew that it ended with 933. He immediately copied the contact, raced down to a business center and dialed it. It was indeed Amina's voice. He quickly announced his name. Before long, Amina arrived at the quadrangle. The two lovers who had missed each other since two years could not control themselves. The way they hugged themselves over and over again created a scene. But they could not care about who was monitoring them. After few minutes' chat, the day's business had to start immediately. Amina led him to both the faculty, departmental, Student Affairs offices for the necessary registrations to be done. Later that day, Amina visited Mka at the NFCS secretariat. There Mka narrated his plight to her and she was very sorry for him. After their discussions, Amina asked him to follow her to her hostel so that he would know where she was living. They had as well scheduled where and when they would meet the following day for the continuation of Mka's registration process.

That night, Amina could not sleep. She knew that Mka was very much worried about the lost of his money and phone. And it was necessary for him to pay his fees before the first week of February so that he could get his Matriculation number and access to the school portal for his online registration of courses and other online activities. Where could they raise about One Hundred and Thirty-Five Thousand Naira that would be enough to clear the debts was her puzzle. She thought of involving her father; but how could dad feel about it? Personally, all she could comfortably bring out from her pocket money was just Fifty Thousand Naira Only. That would not solve the problem. At that point, a thought came to her. She had to go together with Mka to the Muslim Students Fellowship. The fellowship has enough money as their senior colleagues would always pay in a reasonable sum into their Bank account every month. But would Mka accept to go? Mka to her who was an Evangelist in the Christendom would not accept to go to the Mosque just because of money. But any way, he has not option she thought.

Very early on Wednesday morning, after the morning prayers in the mosque, Amina met the Imam, narrated the story of her friend to him and finally pleaded with him to lend her some money to help her friend. The Imam could not give his words that morning. He told Amina to come with Mka in the evening so that they would explain to the whole executive about what she needed from the fellowship. Mka who had believed and was waiting on the Holy Spirit as Bro Bode had advised him was elated to know that Amina had taken a very big step towards solving his problem. But going to the Mosque, he thought was a very big challenge to him. He told Amina that he would call her before evening to tell her if he would go to the Mosque with her or not. But before then, he heartily thanked Amina so much for loving him that much.

When he got to the NFCS secretariat that afternoon, he told Bro Bode, Sis Uyime. Sis Binta, Bro. Joshua and Sis. Mary who were all executive members of the fellowship the offer he had from Amina. Bro. Bode advised him to decline the offer. He narrated to him the story of one Born Again Christian: Sis Rosaline who "was so strong in the lord. One day, Sis. Rosaline fell sick and was taken to the hospital. But unfortunately, the doctor could not discover any sickness on her. She was taken to about four different specialist hospitals, but none could give a tangible cause of her illness after diagnosis. As such, her people were frustrated and had to keep her at home for the Lord to do his will in her condition. One day, a neighbor visited and said that she knew of a man who could cure Sis. Rosaline. Both her husband and her children all were willing to let in the man so far as the illness would be healed. But when Sis. Rosaline knew that the arrangement was to invite a native doctor to heal her, she declined. The sickness had to linger and got to a very worst state. One day, Sis. Rosaline was in comatose; she did not know that her husband had invited the native doctor who did some incantations with some coins. After which, Sis. Rosaline's hand was placed on the coins before the native doctor could continue his medications. After everything done, it was finally discovered that she was dead. Her soul was seen travelling on a very straight road. When she got to a junction, she heard people screaming from one end, while on the other end, she heard people singing and rejoicing. Sis. Rosaline had to turn over to go to the side where she was hearing people singing. To her, that was the way to paradise. But immediately she wanted to make a step, a very ugly black man with a tale and horns appeared to her and told her that she belonged to the hell fire. But Sis. Rosaline could not believe him; she told him how she had been a Born Again Christian on earth and how she had led many people to Christ. When she felt that she had vindicated herself with her confessions, the devil brought out a coin and showed her; asking her if she knew anything about the coin. He further told her that it was a devilish coin that was brought to her by the native doctor, and having touched the coin when she was alive, Sis Rosaline had sold her soul to the devil. As such, the paradise was no longer for her. As the devil tried to drag her to the Hell Fire, a Whiteman on a white robe appeared. He was Jesus who saved Sis. Rosaline and sent her back to the world to amend her ways and tell people to be careful of where and how they get help in times of trouble".

Bro Bode told Mka that accepting anything from the Muslims who were uncircumcised people was tantamount to selling one's soul to the devil. As such, he concluded that Mka should resist Amina's offer. The whole thing put Mka in a dilemma. He did not know what next to do. It was already 2:30pm and if he missed going to the Mosque with Amina by 4pm, he would keep waiting till when the Holy Spirit would finally decided to send him manner from above as Bro Bode advised him. As he was ruminating on this, he had a trance. In that trance, he heard a voice that told him to use his head and never let anything deceive him. As if that was not enough, he was walking in that trance when he saw a beautiful cashew fruit well ripped. He wanted to go and pluck it, but his friends were telling him that if he does, bees would sting him. When he finally decided not to go for the fruit, someone else went and plucked it without any bee stinging him. After eating the fruit, the person told him to go home and read Acts 10: 13-16. Immediately after that, the person disappeared and Mka woke up. It was 3:50pm. He picked and opened his bible to the quotation he had gotten in the dream. On seeing what the passage says, Mka immediately washed his face and went to Amina's hostel. Amina was waiting for him. She was running out of patience as time was no longer on their side. They immediately left for the Mosque. Mka was not at ease being in the Mosque. He could neither understand the language of the prayers not the whole system of worship. It was indeed amusing to him, but he dare not laugh it out as that would be detrimental. After the prayers that evening, Amina and Mka went to the secretariat where after discussion with the executive, they decided to unconditionally give Mka the sum of One Hundred Thousand Naira. It was indeed mind-blowing. To Mka, the world was just defined in paradox. What and where people condemn is their source of life. Tolu a Yoruba, NFCS a Roman Catholic fellowship, Amina an Hausa and a Muslim and other personal experiences showed him that life is more than what a worm's eyes can see

Mka had happily paid all his fees, the matriculation has come and gone. It was then time for the academic work to set in properly. The days were going and he was feeling more indebted and in love with Amina. He has never in life told her that he loved her. They just saw themselves as best of friends. Mka was having the urge to move the relationship to another level. But two major things were his fears. The first one was that he was not ready for a serious relationship. He was a virgin who believed that all the favour he was getting from people including Amina was because of his covenant with God. The second reason was that Amina was a Muslim. He was not sure if both parents would support the inter religious marriage. Due to these two reasons, Mka found it difficult to open up to Amina to tell her how much he loved her.

One Sunday evening, Mka had visited Amina in her hostel. He told her that he could not stay long with her because he had a seminar presentation the following day. But before he could leave, he handed her an envelope. After some seconds of Mka's departure, Amina opened it to see what was inside it. She brought out a well written poem from it that read thus

This feeling is getting too much; yes, it is getting too tight.

The feeling to dance to the tune of Eros, I have pondered all nights.

Attempts to conquer my psyche, rather repulsed my coyness

Thus, in lewd-chastity, my whole being was engulfed.

Nexus or isolation, the dual concepts of my night became haunting.

Oh! To what decision my morning light will dawn?

My emotional battle I thought was only nocturnal, but the dawn calls it a mirage.

The days' chore made an introduction, and exposed me to cathedral of damsels.

Distinct but all glamorous they stand in peculiar postures that worth admiration.

In a knit I am with them, but an abstract Sahara of vastness exists.

The consummation of the ecstasy on ones' breast is what l envisage.

But then, my Gordian knot lacks its Alexander.

In my heart of hearts, I wish to start by splashing my status quo.

Thus, in our entire ambience, to match a mutual rhythm.

Firstly, a coy and soft ride that will predate a 'licit –amour'.

Then, youthful hues that fascinate our rough ride for the globe is racing.

In the flowery Eden we will place our bed with obedience to the maker.

This illusion is my equation to solve, but a slave to myself I remain.

Chastity with its hegemonic influence is retaining me in bondage.

Being the laboratory and reagent, nature I see contradicts itself.

Morality and chastity the pulpit professes, but nature places contradictory force.

Oh! In dilemma I am now, solution is what I long for.

Isolation or nexus, which one?

She read the poem for several times. She really knew that Mka loved her, but it confuses her that Mka could not open up. But through the poem, she knew certain things she had hitherto not known. Mka's poem made her loved him more. She did not know Mka was a poet and of course a very intelligent and skillful one. That night, she had a million dreams and Mka featured in all of them. So was Mka on his own side.

The following day, Mka had gone to his department at 9:55am. His seminar presentation was supposed to start at 11am. He wanted to do some revision before the presentation. Sitting on the quadrangle, he saw Amina coming. He was very shy as he knew that the poem must be connected with her coming. To him, he may have fucked up by writing such poem to her. But there was nothing he could do again, as she was fast approaching. Amina told him how good the poem was, but in order not to distract him from his revision; she told him that they would have to meet later that evening in her hostel. But Mka objected that it should be in Chittis. Chittis is a popular eatery in the school.

Later that evening, Mka was in Chittis as early as 4pm waiting for his date. Within the next ten minutes of his arrival, Amina joined him. She has not been as beautiful as she was that day. Amina wore a purple Italian braided gown. With shoe and hand bag to match the colour. Mka knew that his female friend was very beautiful, but not as much as Amina appeared that day. They shook hands in a way of welcoming each other as Amina sat. Mka requested to know what she would take, which she said would be a plate of jollof rice with a bottle of chilled coke. That was very small compared to what Mka had expected. Mka told the waitress to serve them two plates of jollof rice and two bottles of chilled coke. After the meal, Amina quickly brought out her purse to pay but Mka who was fast enough noticed what she wanted to do, he quickly brought out One Thousand Naira from his wallet and paid the waitress. He has vowed that if there is nothing he could do for Amina, let it be that he paid for her lunch that day. Amina thanked him for both the meal and the poem. They spent much time discussing the poem and how each of them has chosen the kind of lifestyle they have chosen. Amina asked him how he used to feel and how he currently feels about Muslims. To Mka, it was a very simple question that was very difficult to answer. Mka told him that to them in the East, they took every Northerner as an Hausa and every Hausa as a Muslim. The Muslims to them are unbelievers who could never make heaven at last. Being a friend to a Muslim simply means being in enmity with God. He further told her that Christians believe that no good thing could come out from Muslim and if a Muslim rules over a Christian both in politics and in other realms of leadership, it simply means that God is angry with the Christians and has decided to punish them with the said Muslim ruler. More so, Muslims to them are murderers who are blood thirsty. That was why the Boko Haram, Al-Qaeda, and other Islamic sects are bent to their crimes said Mka. "Okay, but now, I am a Muslim, and we are friends. What can you say about the religion now using both me and other Muslims you have come in contact with?" Dear what else do you want me to say if not telling you exactly whom you are. You are the Islamic religion I know, and right now, you are the best human I know on earth so what other explanation do you want from me? The only thing is that in any gathering of people, there are always good ones and bad ones. Nothing more", said Mka. So what about you, what can you say about the Christianity as you have known it before and as you know it now?" Mka asked. "My dear, like what you people have about us, I used to think that Christians are nothing but weaklings who got their weakness from Jesus Christ and his teaching. For example, Jesus Christ was so weak that he had to die in the hands of ordinary mortal sinners. He also urged his adherents not to defend themselves rather give their second cheek for a second slap. Christians are also infidels who must be brought to Allah by conversion, but if they prove stubborn, the use of force must be employed. This is done by what we call Jihad. We believe that there is no reason why people should not turn to Allah. We have decided to force those who have not seen the light to enter even if they are blind. But note that most people abuse this part of our belief. Christians are seen as idolaters. They do not worship one god; instead they have their allegiance to God the Father, God the Son, God the Holy Spirit and Virgin Mary. So to us, Christians are confused and even within the religion, there are different factions who do not believe in the systems of the others. The bible which is the holy book of the Christian religion is contradicting. It has many chapters against each other, supporting feminism, and so on" said Amina. But now, I think we have so many wrong perceptions about the religion. Here on campus, I have seen good Christians and have mingled with them. I have come to know that most of these views are from shallow-minded bigots. Using you as an example, I have gotten to know that not all male Christians are amorous, selfish and so on."

"But Amina can you marry a Christian especially one from another ethnic group from yours?" asked Mka. Amina laughed and paused for a while "Do you want to marry me? She asked. "Anyway, my dad is a Muslim Cleric and I don't believe he would want his daughter to be married by someone other than from his religion.

This is common in our religion. Our ladies are hardly allowed to be married by Christians, but for our men marrying Christian women, it is highly permissible because the lady would definitely become a Fidel. Well, to answer your question, based on my level of exposure, I do not think that I would marry religion, ethnic group and so on. I would marry a man I love, a man that would love me, a man who could give me everything a wife deserves. Nothing more, nothing less. But I am not saying I am marrying Mka Odu ooo", she answered. "Please Mka lets change the topic; let us talk about me. You have not said anything about my dress. I expected you to appreciate me but you are a clumsy boy. So I am not beautiful right? Now I know that I either have a blind friend or a misogynist" she bantered on Mka. After a deep laugh, Mka told her that he really appreciated her beauty and how much he has been lusting and admiring her beauty since they entered the eatery. He finally promised her that he would send her a poem describing her through Facebook message later in the day. It was already late, they had to leave for their homes.

Mka was satisfied that night. That was the first outing he had had with a woman. More so, buying lunch for Amina was a very big achievement for him. He could not sleep as the thought of Amina engulfed him. When he finally dozed off, he dreamt of her all through the night. He could not wake till around 7am of the following day. He then picked his phone, and sent a poem to Amina via Facebook chat. It was the message beep of her phone that woke Amina that morning. She opened it, and it read

"In a trance was l this morning when l heard sparrows chanting harmoniously.

Ecstatically, l gazed towards my window; behold the peeping sun from the East. The rays were illuminating and finding their way through my window.

As l tried but could not behold the rays, l began to think about anything that shares the same quality with the sun.

After some minutes of my psychic rumination, recalled my mind of someone.

I began to describe this entity to myself. It was then that l realized that even the morning sun emulates her in terms of brightness...

These were the things that formed the reminiscent of my ponder-

Her smile is a persimmon and brings radiance to the grief and epitomizes a dazzling gazelle.

Her angelic eyes charm and glitter more than the sun in its action.

Her loosely hanging and dangling breasts can seduce the misogynist. Their succulence is quintessential to the xerophytes. Their erected posture is a macrocosm to an erected vein of the promiscuous cromagnum. The nipples attract like the magnet.

All over her physique rested youthful hues like the morning dew in grassland. A perfect contour engulfed her like the Jerusalem Mountain.

I can only define this exceptional damsel in microcosm.

Thus, after beholding her pulchritude, my quest to have a nexus with her grew vaster than the Sahara and deeper than the Atlantic. I began to envisage that garden where Adamic love was played...

But all was a mirage because of my modus-operandi.

Guess who she is..."

"OMG! This guy is something else" she screamed as she jumped out of her bed to show her roommate the message. "It was indeed wonderfully constructed" said Durah. "Don Allah nuna mani yaron cewa ya rubuta wannan" (please show me the boy that wrote this) requested Durah in Hausa language. "Clap for yourself, smart girl. You want to snatch my boyfriend from me right? Better go and get one for yourself. No vacancy in my Mka's heart. But Durah, am I that beautiful or is this guy flattering me. Look at what he wrote about my eyes, my boobs, and my physique in fact my whole self. I don't think I am this beautiful or am I?" asked Amina. "Of course babe, you are very beautiful. Or do you think that all these calls that I receive always are for me alone? Hmmm. Some of them are your admirers telling me to help them convince you ooo. But this Igbo boy must be very lucky to have your heart this much." said Durah. After the discussion, Amina called Mka and the following conversations took place.

Mka: Hello, who is on the line? Do I know you?

Amina: No, you don't know me; let me tell you whom I am. I am a torment who was sent by the spirit world to emotionally torment one Mr. Mka Odu.

Mka: that could be a coincidence. My name is Mka and I belong to a brotherhood that gave me the assignment to die in the hands of a lady called Amina. So now that we can help ourselves, how do we meet?

Amina: naughty dude. How was your night Jaree?

Mka: It was so awesome. I had good time with my mistress the previous day, and the thought of her took me all through the night. So it was indeed cool for me.

Amina: Good to know that. Mka that lady on your poem most be exceptionally beautiful with the description you gave her. I think she should be the most beautiful woman on earth. Please I have an advice for you: do everything you can, to marry her ooo. She is cool and she needs you to do that soon.

Mka: lol. Thanks for appreciating her. But I asked

you to guess whom she is...oya whom do you think she is?

Amina: Who else is she if not Amina Mustafa. The woman that loves you more than you could imagine. A woman that can let go of anything just to have you as a husband. Mka the lady loves you with her life.

Mka: wow! That is so cool. I also love her so dearly. She is my world. She positively changed my perceptions on many things. She made me the student I am today. She is my muse. She spurs out the best in me. Because of her, I have decided to work as hard as humanly possible to make money, marry her and make her the best wife in the world. I also wish to have the happiest family in the world with her. We would make the most beautiful children in the world. I have many good things to do with her, and as long as there is life, I believe I would make it with her.

Amina: (breathe heavily) I am speechless. I pray things work out for you and her. She would be happier than you. Mka can we chat later? I have to go and prepare for lectures. Bye

Mka: bye!

Two years has passed since Mka entered the university. He has been growing in faith. He loved his membership to NFCS. His devotion to the fellowship has earned him the post of the Prayer Secretary. Among other things Mka has done as the prayer secretary was organizing evangelisms to both within and outside the university. Mka was surprised that as now a Roman Catholic, he could still speak in tongues. He could still pray and people would fall under the anointing. He could still pray and God would answer his prayers. All these were things he thought were never possible for the Catholics. But even at this level of conviction, Mka was still not at ease with saying the Rosary. To him, it was nothing but idolatry. But who was he to question God. If he could say prayers even with the rosary and get his prayers answered, there was nothing to worry about.

By April that year, NFCS had a national convention to attend at University of Ibadan. The convention was going to last from Thursday through Sunday. Unfortunately for Mka, he had an exam on Friday. He could not imagine leaving his exams for a convention. He really had to attend the convention. Right from his first day in the fellowship, Mka has been told that God could do everything. As the prayer secretary too, he was one of those preaching and telling younger students that there was nothing impossible for God to do. So for him not to attend the convention would be tantamount to not practicing what he preaches. So he decided to pray for God to cause the lecturer to postpone the examination. Mka and the team of NFCS had prayed fervently and have received prophecies during their prayers telling them that God has settled the case. They would not have to be afraid of anything. So because of the assurance, on Thursday that day, Mka confidently led others to the convention at Ibadan.

It was indeed a wonderful time with the Lord. The convention which was attended by all the Catholic Students Fellowship all over Nigeria featured great men of God both from within and outside the country.

By Sunday, the convention was over and the ABU team had successfully gotten back to the campus. Mka was so desperate to hear that his exam did not hold. But contrary to what he expected, the exam took place as planned. But he was still hopeful. God still works in a mysterious way and he has done it for many brethren before. He would not change during Mka's time. Sis. Binta had shared the testimony of a brother who could not write his final year exam because he went for Morning Cry the day the exam was supposed to hold. But because he was working in the lord's vineyard, when the result came out, he made the best result out an exam he never wrote. This testimony boosted Mka's morale. He resorted to prayers telling God to see reasons why he would pass him miraculously. Throughout the Easter holiday, Mka soaked himself in prayers for God to do wonders for him when the results would be out.

Second semester has arrived, that would be the last semester Amina had to stay as an undergraduate of the ABU. As such, she was busy with her B.Sc. Project work. As for Mka, his concern was the result of the previous semester. Within the first three weeks, the results were out. Mka made As and Bs on all the courses he had seen so far. The last to come out was PHIL 311. It was indeed the one Mka was expecting miracle from God. Before long, the result was out. Mka could not believe what he saw. That was the first time he had an F since he entered the university. When he got to the secretariats, he told the other NFCS executive members what fate befell him. They were sorry for him, but still had to remind him that nothing happens without God knowing why. They told him that God had better plans for him ahead. Mka had to sit for the exam the following academic year.

## CHAPTER SEVEN

# THE CLASH OF THE STATUS QUO

**RIGHT DEEP** inside of him, Mka was very angry and disappointed in himself. Considering his level, he believed that no one could deceive him with cheap religious teaching. But there he was being denied of his thirst to be the best graduating student of his department. He could not blame God because as an evangelist, he had preached on the issue of time. He had read from Ecclesiastics chapter three that there was time for everything. More so, he could not blame the other members of the NFCS who advised him about what had happened.

Having blamed himself for his foolishness, Mka decided to be more concentrated on his studies than before. To the other fellowship members, Bro. Mka

Odu was gradually backsliding. He needed more prayers from the brethren than ever before, they concluded.

Amina on her own side was busy with her B.Sc. research work. She had discovered that her friend was psychologically unhealthy. It was unlike him and she did everything within her reach to make him happy. But all was a futile effort. Mka had never told her that he had an F because of misplaced priority and has decided to give himself some weeks of exile which involved not going to his department apart from during lecture periods, paying little attention to friends, and non-involvement in any activity that would take him outside the NFCS Secretariat.

One day, Amina visited Mka without an invitation. That was the first time she could do that. Before he could get to the door, Sis. Uyime had seen her. Seeing Amina made her very angry because they believed that Mka was falling away from the faith because of his friendship with the Muslim girl. Sis Uyime quickly went and informed other members of the fellowship present that Amina was coming to see Mka. They quickly agreed that Sis. Uyime should tell her that Mka was not around. Amina left very angry. She had neither seen nor heard from Mka for the past two days. His phone was off too. To her, it was like two centuries that she has not seen Mka. As she was going home, she sensed that Mka was inside; but how sure was she. She went home very angry that day. If not for Durah's intervention, she could not have eaten that night. She was like someone that lost her husband. The following morning, as early as 6:30am, there was a knock on the NFCS secretariat door. When Sis. Mary opened the door, it was Amina. She was looking very disturbed as she inquired about Mka. Though Sis. Mary was very sorry for her, but she could not tell her that Mka was in. She told her that Mka went for a zonal convention to Kano. To Amina, that was a blatant lie. Mka could hardly leave his room without informing her of his way about. How come he suddenly travelled to as far distance as Kano without letting her know. But all these were her thought. She thanked Mary for attending to her and left.

Durah could not continue seeing her friend in such a depressed state. Amina had spent the whole day in the Philosophy Department asking after Mka, but everyone she asked was having the same testimony. Mka has not been to the department for a while. Durah then decided to help her out. She had sensed along Amina that the NFCS knew Mka's way about and had decided to separate them. But one thing they could not explain was why Mka could not call Amina on phone at least to tell her that their friendship was over. Durah who was not known by anyone in the fellowship decided to go for Mka the following day. When she knocked at the NFCS door, Bro. Solomon came out. She told him that she was Mka's course mate and had not seen Mka in the department for some days. She claimed that a seminar topic was shared and that she was paired together with Mka. Bro Solomon excused himself to call Mka who came out and was surprised to see Durah instead of one of his course mates as Solomon had told him. But he could not let Bro. Solomon know his surprise. After greetings, Durah handed him a letter Amina had written. On the letter, Amina had queried Mka on what her crime was. Why he had wanted her to commit suicide. She further explained to Mka the number of times she had visited without seeing him. She finally reminded Mka the chat they had after their date in Chittis where Mka told her how much he loved and would cherish her. After reading the letter, Mka put on his phone and sent her a text telling her to wait for him in their hostel's quadrangle by 4pm that evening.

When Durah got home that morning, she was surprised by what she saw. Amina was jubilating like someone who had worn a ticket to Jannah. As soon as she saw Durah, she ran and hugged her. The speed at which she ran to her made both of them to stagger uncontrollably. "Amina are you alright? Has Mka caused you madness? Please take it easy ooo. Ba haka ne aki koana (this is not how to be in love)" said Durah. "Durah you are a genius. How did you do it? Guess what, Mka sent me a message some minutes before you came in. He said he would come to see me at 4pm" explained

Amina. It was indeed a good news, but Durah could not believe that a mere promise to visit her could make her to get lost in such euphoria of happiness.

At exactly 4pm, Amina raced down to the quadrangle. She was surprised to see Mka already seated waiting for her. She just pretended as if she did not see him. When she entered the quadrangle, she went and sat in the opposite direction without even greeting him. When Mka greeted, she could not respond. The only word she could utter was to tell him to just say what he came to say or else she would leave. Mka really knew that she deserved an apology. He did not hesitate to apologize. Amina who was feigning her attitude turned her face away from Mka meaning that she was not giving heed to the apology. Mka had to leave his seat, went and sat beside her, touched her hair and say "babe you are so beautiful. I did not mean to frustrate you. I decided to turn-off my phone in order not to talk to you in annoyance. Someone like you does not deserve to be answered in an angry state". He kept touching her hair softly, down to her neck, and pecked her neck. Amina was nearly frozen by the peck. It was the most sensual Amina had received in her entire life. And receiving that from Mka added flavour to it. Amina looked him in his eyes and said, "Mka I love you with the last drop of my blood. You are disturbed, and you want me to be happy. How do you think that would be possible? My happiness is you and you are my happiness. Please tell me why you have been angry for days now. Tell me what I have done wrong. Is it because I am a Muslim? Mka I can denounce my faith to make you happy. I can even elope if my father try to be a hindrance between us. Tell me why you have been sad for days". With the look on Amina's face, her eyes, her beauty and the words she had just said to Mka, even the Lucifer could repent. "Dearie you have done no bad to me. Since I have known you, I have not gotten any regret of knowing you. You have been my pedestal and happiness. I was just the cause of my mood. I took a very wrong decision last semester, and the outcome of it is haunting me. I had an F last semester". Amina was surprised to hear that. Mka of all people can never have an F even if he entered the hall ten minutes before the exam could finish. But she was not out to start blaming him for that. She instead told him that failing exams is one of what makes a student. People fail exams not spirits. She tried to make her boy come up to himself again. She stood from the seat and sat on Mka's lap and was softly touching his beards as she told him not to worry. She spoke happiness and strength into him. "Dearie I dey H. would you mind coming into my room so that we'd eat together? I have not eaten since yester night because I was missing you so much". Mka could not resist her request as they walked into the room. Durah was pleased to see Amina happy again on Mka's arms. She offered Mka seat after they exchanged peasantries. "Durah you dey lie well well ooo. I know it was this lover daughter of Mustafa that made you do that", said Mka. "Wait wait wait don't insult my Father ooo. Address him with some respect for he is the strongest man on earth. Do you think that an any-how man can give birth to a daughter that could win Mka's heart? Please give him some credit by adding that little Alhaji to his name" interrupted Amina. The two lovers could not allow Durah to say a word as they were throwing banter at each other. It was after some minutes that Mka told Amina how Durah had skillfully told Bro. Solomon that she was his course mate who visited because of seminar delivery.

That night was indeed fun for the three students. Mka enjoyed the meal of tuwo shinkafa that Durah served him and Amina. It was getting late, and Mka had to take his leave. But before he could leave, Amina insisted that they would meet the following day. They agreed to meet in school at Philosophy department's quadrangle at 4pm.

At the quadrangle, Mka narrated the event that led to his historic F on PHIL 311 exam. Amina was not at ease with the cause. She had imagined that the result was either because the lecturer may have decided to fail Mka or that another student copied verbatim from Mka. She, therefore, scolded him by telling him that Allah was not that stupid and a magician who could pass Mka on an exam he never wrote. She further argued that it would be unjust for Allah to cause the exam to be postponed just because Mka was not ready for it while thousand other innocent students would be disorganized. She continued by telling him that he failed to use his time judiciously which was a big sin in the Islamic religion. To them (Muslims), she explained, Allah is an organized being who takes timing very serious. Similarly, every man has to do same. To the believers, it is the biggest asset which can be converted into other benefits including passing exams. Time to them is not gold rather life and if anyone misuses any given time, Allah never takes it lightly with such person because it would be detrimental to the defaulter's Eeman. She further enumerated that in Islamic worldview, the importance of timing oneself is so important that Muslims were bid to work towards ensuring benefiting from time, utilizing leisure time, Racing for good deeds, learning from the passage of time, Seeking the superior times, Planning and organizing time, Fulfillment of time commitments, Necessary awareness of time wasters. She also added that the Qur'an and the Sunnah enjoin Muslims to be conscious of time, value it for the satisfaction of Allah. For the guidance and success of everyone. One must never waste time nor abuse it…Islam encourages Muslims to care for time, to utilize it wisely and not to waste it and to benefit from it. Besides, it holds them responsible for their time. As such, Mka who never took his timing as serious as it should be taken should now be responsible for his injudiciousness, she added. She also told Mka that every minute of one's life matters a lot from one second to a whole year. To buttress this, she said "To realize the value of one year, ask a student who has failed a grade. To realize the value of one month, ask a mother who has given birth to a premature baby. To realize the value of one week, ask an editor of a weekly newspaper. To realize the value of one day, ask a daily wage labourer who has kids to feed. To realize the value of one hour, ask the lovers who are waiting to meet. To realize the value of one minute, ask a person who has missed a train. To realize the value of one second, ask a person who has avoided an accident. To realize the value of one mili-second, ask the person who has won a silver medal in the Olympics.

Amina spoke an immeasurable sense into him. But instead of ruminating on her speech as it concerns him and his education, he was lost in the juxtaposition of the Islamic views as espoused by Amina and what the Christians believe about time. Everything Amina just finished telling him is summarized in the book of Ecclesiastics chapter three. He also thought of the good examples of the sons of Isachar in Acts 19 whom the holy bible says understood the time. As he pondered on the similarities he has seen in the two religious groups, he was far lost in thought to him, the Muslims, Christians, Animists, Judaists and other religious groups cannot be correct at the same time. This his thought was borne out of what each of the groups preaches. They all believed that theirs is the right and there was no other religion that could lead one to the One True God and the eternal bliss that would be enjoyed in the paradise at the end of the world. Even at this his belief, Mka also bent on Bertrand Russel's position when the later wrote that "but for my part, I cannot see any ground for either. I do not pretend to be able to prove that there is no God. I equally cannot prove that Satan is a fiction. The Christian God may exist; so may the Gods of Olympus, or ancient Egypt, or of Babylon. But no one of these hypotheses is more probable than any other: they lie outside the region of even probable knowledge, and therefore there is no reason to consider any of them". Yes, of all these religious groups that are eminent in Nigeria: Christianity, Islam, African Traditional Religion, Mka has had encounter with them at one point or another. He has not forgotten the story his father told him He had heard from his father how Amadioha was just and faithful to fight justly for him before his birth.

But in the face of the seeming rightness of these religious groups, Mka has had some convictions within him that the Christian religion is the ultimate way to God. But the more he tried to be fully convinced on this, the more he repulsed his thought. He has seen that even Christianity is a hydra-headed religion with the denominations disagreeing to agree among themselves. This is so because he has been an Anglican from his childhood. He spent most of his life time from one

Anglican institution or the other. He has seen the true work of God in the Anglican church. The favor he has been receiving from his childhood has been out of what he learnt from the Anglican church. As an Anglican, he has as well believed that the Roman Catholics are very far from the kingdom. They could not receive the holy spirit, as they do not believe wholly in the bible as the only way to God. They have included in their "Catechism of Christian Doctrine, number eleven question where it was asked "How are you to know what God has revealed?" in answering it, they held that "I am to know what God has revealed by the testimony, teaching, and authority of the Catholic Church" As an Anglican, Mka had believed that this doctrine made it glaring that the Roman Catholic placed her authority over the bible. Another point of reference as Mka remembered was the number hundredth question which asked "Can the Church err in what she teaches?" The answer has it that "The church cannot err in what she teaches as to faith or morals, for she is our infallible guide in both". Regarding this, Mka recalled what Aunty Ocha taught him about the apostles in Galatians 1:8 and 9, and in second epistle of John chapter 10. He learnt that any other person or doctrine that teaches any other thing is ungodly. More so, Mka remembered what he read in Bertrand Russell's Why I Am Not A Christian. How the papacy was believed to be extra humans who are infallible. It is believed that the Roman Catholics also resort to incessant hiding of the truth from their adherents. For instance, the Roman Catholic opposed Galileo, Darwin, Freud and others. He also remembered that he had read that Pope Gregory the Great had written a letter to a certain bishop saying, "A report has reached us which we cannot mention without a blush, that thou expoundest grammar to certain friends". From his analysis of this, Mka concluded that the Church reserved knowledge and truth to certain social class of people.

Catholics were also believed to be deceiving themselves with the belief in the purgatory and the worshipping of the queen of heaven whom they call the Virgin Mary and the dead whom they call saints. This worship system, according to what Mka had learnt in the Anglican church, contravene the Second Commandment. They were seen as having other gods in place of the true God. As such, it is argued that the Catholics would end up in the Sulphuric hell with the devil.

But contrary to Mka's previous belief that the Catholics are damned people as they have bought for themselves express ticket to hell through their belief systems and the fact that the Holy Spirit is not in the Church, Mka has been a member of NFCS and that has given him some views about the true nature of the Catholic church. He has seen that there is the Holy Spirit in the Church, Catholics still have moral upright people like the Anglicans. He refused to believe everything he had heard about them Though he was confused with why the same God could be in the Roman and Anglican churches who are different in many ways.

As Mka battle within him to settle the Anglo-Catholic question, the thought of other denominations within the religion rear their heads up. He imagined their pros and cons. For instance, he has remembered his encounter with a Jehovah Witness at Rowa in 2011. He has learnt that the Witnesses do not believe in the concept of Trinity as they rightly hold that the word cannot be seen anywhere in the bible. They also discard the beliefs in the Hell Fire, the second coming of Christ, the everlasting nature of Satan, the ungodliness of such events as the widely celebrated Christmas, and so on. The Seventh Day Adventism too, Mka recalled believed in the strict adherence to the Ten Commandments. As such, they hold that in order to please God, one has to observe the Sabbath day without any compromise. And Sabbath day is on Saturdays, as such those who worship on days other than the Saturdays are worshipping the European gods.

When Mka thought through all these, juxtaposed them with his personal experience as an Anglican at home, a Catholic on campus and other relationships he had had with other members of the different denominations in the Christendom, he got more confused. What obfuscated him most was that God would always hear the prayers of each of these groups who see themselves as right and others wrong.

After a while, his memory ran through what he knew about the African Traditional Religion. He reasoned that people were living in Africa even before the coming of the external religions. How and who sustained these people before then if not their ancestral belief and worship system? He also remembered that as an Anglican, he was taught that the ATR believed in a supreme God whom they believed created everything. But their idea of these God was cloudy. They had to resort to worshipping objects, thinking that those things were the agents of their supreme God. Mka reasoned that the worship of the natural creatures which the ATR were accused of, was not different from the Rosary and the Statuses in the Roman Catholic churches, the Cross in the altars of the Anglican and the Catholic churches, the use of candles and so on in the various denominations of the Christendom. The issue of ancestral worship which the ATR were accused of, to him was the same thing as veneration of the Virgin Mary in the Roman Catholic Church, the Saints in both the Roman Catholic and the Anglican Churches. Mka thought that the difference between the ATR and the Christianity was that the ATR venerate the African ancestors while the Christians venerate the European, Asian and American ancestors. Having quickly pondered on all he knew of the ATR,

Mka concluded that the major difference between it and the Christianity is that while the ATR is dominated by African cultural practices, Christianity, on the other hand, leans on the European cultural practices and beliefs. And to him, none can be said to be bad; both cultures are good for the adherents.

As for the Islamic religion, Mka thought there was nothing he needed to know about it as everything has been shown since his meeting with Amina. As an Anglican, he was taught among other things that the Muslims would not be saved at the end because they believed that they could work out their salvation. This their belief made them to labour without comfort. They worship to save themselves not to serve God, and this belief is wrong. Salvation as he knew could only come by grace. As a child, he was also taught that the Quran was not inspired by God. It was written by radicals who needed a document to support their clandestine murderous activities in the name of Jihad. The Islam as he has hither known was also the agent of the Proverbial Anti-Christ and the notorious 666 number. That was why as a Christian, both when he was an Evangelist and now, he was in the University, they have never met to pray without raining fire and the brimstone on the Muslims. They would always tell the Christian God to deal, expose, burn, confuse and do other manner of maltreatments to the Muslims. Apart from the aforementioned, there were other manner of evil things he had heard of the religion. But contrary to the inhuman paintings he had gotten, his experience as a student in the Northern Nigeria, the favour he got from the religion in his first year, the whole thing he had known about Amina Mustafa, he was lost in thought. He regretted participating in a State wide prayer rain organized by Christian Association of Nigeria, Imo State chapter while he was still a child. During that prayer rain, the whole Christians irrespective of denomination gathered and prayed for seven days against 'Herod' whom they said was the Muslim. It was on issues like this that the Christians gather in unity without denominational quagmires coming into play. From the day Mka met, Amina who was a strong Muslim, he regretted asking his God to deal with Muslims. He believed that it was tantamount to laying abuses and courses on innocent people.

Amina had finished what she was telling Mka and was expecting him to say something. But there was a grave silence from him. She gazed at his face and discovered that Mka may not been listening to what she has been saying. She shook his head. It was then that Mka who seemed absent minded responded shockingly. "I am sorry dear, I have heard everything you said, and I am going to make good use of my time as you have advised. Thanks a lot for your concern and all you have done towards my welfare". Mka said as they stood to leave.

Mka got to the NFCS secretariat not being himself. To him, he would not have rest that night till he sorts himself out. He believed that it was time for him to believe things not because of what he was taught. To him, his Sunday school teachers like other teachers taught what they want their students to know not what the students need to know. He believed that most times, the minds of the students are smothered, stunted, reformatted and filled with all manner of heretical lies. He rhetorically asked himself "which is better: believing on others' beliefs, theories and teachings without trying to verify the validity of such beliefs, theories and teachings or seeking for the 'truth' and unveiling the truth even when it hurts?. He believed that his mind has been in prison and must be liberated. As this line of thought came into him, not minding that it was night, he decided to go to the philosophical garden of Eden. He needed no one to interrupt his taught. But he knew that Amina would call and she would not be at ease if she calls and fails to get him. Therefore, before he could go, he called Amina and informed her that his phone battery was almost flat. He finally wished her a pleasant night rest. He switched off his phone and went to the philosophical garden of Eden.

It was indeed a sweet night. The moon was so bright that one could pick a pin from the ground. With the trees and flowers at the philosophical garden of the Eden, and birds chirping, Mka was so relaxed. He had said his prayers because to him, trying to know the truth can never be against God. He thus urged God to reveal himself to him that night. After that, he took himself round to everything he knew about any religion of the world. He has seen both the good and the bad things in all of them. As he was lost in thought, he saw himself enjoying some abstract food. He tried to decipher what the meal was, but he could not. As he wanted to leave the food he was enjoying, he discovered that he could not go beyond a particular place. Before he could know what was happening, he was thrown into great fear. He started screaming so loudly but it seemed no one could hear him. Fortunately, a mighty wind blew open the cage and entered a man who wanted to lead him out. Immediately the man stretched forth his hand to lead him out, Mka woke and saw his department security man dragging him up from where he was lying. "kai, wetin dey do me? what I kwom here vis time to do? I hear my cry vrom za gate I kwome za see wetin dey happen to me; I see me dancing for grand wen I kwome. Tell me what I dey do me before I shoot me now" said Aliyu the security man. Mka could not utter any word. He was very much terrified with the nightmare. When Aliyu finally discovered that it was Mka, he calmed down because he knew him as one of the brightest students of the department. Mka pleaded with him to accompany him home as he claimed that he has forgotten the way home. Without any hesitation, Aliyu led him home. It was 12:55am. The other people living at the NFCS have been looking for him. They were surprised to see Mka led home by a security man. Different thoughts took over their minds. While some where thinking that he was drugged by Amina, others were thinking that he may have been beaten by some coult guys. Aliyu had gone, and Mka could hardly utter a word. He instead was twerking and whirling restlessly on the floor. None could sleep that night till around 3:15am when Mka slept. But even at that, Sis Uyime refused to go to bed. Uyime had been crushing on Mka for a very long time. But to her, Mka has been turning down her green light because of the Muslim trap he had entered in Amina. She had decided to monitor him till dawn.

By 6am, all were awake including Mka. When he was asked what happened to him the previous night, Mka who was subconscious started reciting some words that were to abstract for them to understand. Among the few that they could hear though not clearly understood by everyone was

"He is in a prison, liberate him for he is in a prison. In a prison he remains inert but he has power. His potency dies while in the prison. He is in a prison, he can't live. In a prison he only exists but not to live.

You-the jailer- are very deceitful and crafty. You claim you are doing him good, but it is a sham. The prison maker saw the light and wouldn't want the prisoner to see. You say it is faith but I call it prison. Your jail denies him many things, fail to tell him everything, but want him to believe without questioning. You want to deceive him. You have said to him: 'you walk by faith not by sight' because you don't want him to see the reality. He is in a prison, liberate him for he is in a prison. Loose him to explore for he is a prisoner. He needs to see and read things for himself. He needs to ask questions. Why not expose him to what you've been exposed to? Give him the holy books to read. Give him the sciences to read. Give him the arts to read. Don't tell him stories, he can read; give him to read and explain to himself.

He is a prisoner; yes, human mind is a prisoner. He wants to ask questions do not restrict him. He has to taste cause and effect; enough of faith. He is a prisoner and he is robbed. Free the mind Mr. Religion for you are the jailer. Your prison you call faith does not explain it all. He is a prisoner and he must be freed"

They were all amazed by the whole thing. As such, they resorted to prayers and sprinkling of the Holy Water on him. As the prayer was going on, Mka fell asleep and never to wake up till 10am. He was then mentally sound. Sis. Uyime was happier than all. She immediately made ready water for him to take his bath and got him something to eat. After the meal, she went to him privately to ask him what the problem was. It was then that Mka had to narrate to her the encounter he had the previous night. Before he could finish the story, other people have joined in the room. They were all amazed because Mka to them was a Joseph. His dreams hardly fail to manifest. "But what do you think this revelation is up to?" asked Bro Solomon. Mka replied that it was not yet the right time to discuss the dream. He referred them to Apostle Paul's statement when the later says that most of the things he never did were for the sake of the elect. He further said that he had objectively begun to look at events differently until he find the truth.

## CHAPTER EIGHT

# HOW MANY PARADISES

**SOME WEEKS** had passed since his experience, Mka's lifestyle had changed drastically. It was few days to exams. Meanwhile, lectures had stopped. Early in the morning, he would go the school Library and would not return until night. He had decided that apart from serious preparations for his exams, he had to carryout a research to clarify himself of some doubts. Although he was taught to believe as a child that spiritual matters cannot be understood using carnal ways, he believed that he has been in the spirit since the night he had a trance. He thought it wise to balance what he had known with scholarly research. Mka had also believed that before he could conclude on the subject of his research, he had to read about other religious groups, possibly, interview people of different belief systems. Amina too would be interviewed. He would go to Amina's hostel for serious discussion. But that would be after exams. By then, Amina would have defended her project. For him, it was Amina that talked him into the thought that has led him into the research. The thought that has made him to be more confused by so many mysteries and dogmas. The thought that has led him to believe that logically, since all the religions of the world are parallel in almost everything, they are all right and wrong in their own ways. His trance some days back has motivated him to action which made him to be neutral to religious membership till he discover the relatively best one. He has believed that in doing this, he had to have a good knowledge of one central thing in all the religions. The concept of paradise to him needed to direct his thought and research on belief system.

The first day of his research, Mka read so many books on the philosophical perception of Paradise. He read the views of Bertrand Russell, Karl Marx and so on. He read that Paradise is an abstract abode used to keep people of a given sect submissive and silent even in cases where they could ask questions. The adherents, who are rid of freethinking faculties read sheepishly, swallow the stories of the paradise without chewing. They have been taught that one has to debase their selves, accept the identity of a miserable sinner so that they would be made pure for the paradise.

After this, he attempted to know the Buddhist

perspective of Paradise. Fortunately for him, he pounced on an article by *Venerable K. Sri Dhammananda Maha Thera* who wrote that "the Buddhist concept of heaven and hell is entirely different from that in other religions. Buddhists do not accept that these places are eternal. It is unreasonable to condemn a man to eternal hell for his human weakness but quite reasonable to give him every chance to develop himself. From the Buddhist point of view, those who go to hell can work themselves upward by making use of the merit that they had acquired previously. There are no locks on the gates of hell. Hell is a temporary place and there is no reason for those beings to suffer there forever.

The Buddha's teaching shows us that there are heavens and hells not only beyond this world, but in this very world itself. Thus the Buddhist conception of heaven and hell is very reasonable. For instance, the Buddha once said, 'When the average ignorant person makes an assertion to the effect that there is a Hell (patala) under the ocean he is making a statement which is false and without basis. The word 'Hell' is a term for painful sensations. 'The idea of one particular ready-made place or a place created by God as heaven and hell is not acceptable to the Buddhist concept.

The fire of hell in this world is hotter than that of the hell in the world-beyond. There is no fire equal to anger, lust or greed and ignorance. According to Buddha, we are burning from eleven kinds of physical pain and mental agony: lust, hatred, illusion sickness, decay, death, worry, lamentation, pain (physical and mental), melancholy and grief. People can burn the entire world with some of these fires of mental discord. From a Buddhist point of view, the easiest way to define hell and heaven is that where ever there is more suffering, either in this world or any other plane, that place is a hell to those who suffer. And where there is more pleasure or happiness, either in this world or any other worldly existence, that place is a heaven to those who enjoy their worldly life in that particular place. However, as the human realm is a mixture of both pain and happiness, human beings experience both pain and happiness and will be able to realize the real nature of life. But in many other planes of existence inhabitants have less chance for this realization. In certain places there is more suffering than pleasure while in some other places there is more pleasure than suffering.

Buddhists believe that after death rebirth can take place in any one of a number of possible existences. This future existence is conditioned by the last thought-moment a person experiences at the point of death. This last thought which determines the next existence results from the past actions of a man either in this life or before that. Hence, if the predominant thought reflects meritorious action, then he will find his future existence in a happy state. But that state is temporary and when it is exhausted a new life must begin all over again, determined by another dominating 'kammic' energy. This repetitious process goes on endlessly unless one arrives at 'Right View' and makes a firm resolve to follow the Noble Path which produces the ultimate happiness of *Nibbana.*

Heaven is a temporary place where those who have done good deeds experience more sensual pleasures for a longer period. Hell is another temporary place where those evil doers experience more physical and mental suffering. It is not justifiable to believe that such places are permanent. There is no god behind the scene of heaven and hell. Each and every person experiences according to his good and bad *kamma.* Buddhist never try to introduce Buddhism by frightening people through hell-fire or enticing people by pointing to paradise. Their main idea is character building and mental training. Buddhists can practice their religion without aiming at heaven or without developing fear of hell".

Mka had also thought of the ATR. He remembered that he had heard nothing about the Paradise in ATR. Their own paradise could at best be described in the concept of reincarnation. More so, in the place of the paradise, what spur the ATR to do good is to make good names here on earth, be healed of sicknesses, maintain good societal life and to avert death. And when one finally dies, one should reincarnate in a better world.

When he finally went to Amina after their exams, they congratulated each other for successfully wrapping up the academic year. They firstly discussed how Amina's project defense went. It was indeed superb from what they discussed, though the result was yet to be seen. After that, Mka told her that as a philosophy student who would be carrying out his B.A. research by the next academic year, he would like to research on the PHILOSOPHICAL CONCEPT OF PARADISE. As such, he asked her what she knew about Paradise especially from the Islamic perspective. In response, she firstly told him the Arabic name of which is Jannah. This she said was the abode of Allah where He would stay eternally with the faithful. Amina further told him that there are seven levels of Jannah. While Allah whose throne is at the highest Jannah would welcome the said faithful there, other God fearing people: Muslims and non-Muslims alike would be at the other six. Describing Jannah, Amina told him that it is a place where the faithfuls would be welcomed by Allah. These faithfuls would enter the Jannah in groups, the first group that will enter would look like the full moon, while the next groupwould be as radiant as the star in the sky. But irrespective of groups, each man would marry two wives as non would be unmarried. Furthermore, that each man in the paradise shall be given seventy-two virgins with swelling breasts and a brimming cup. And each man irrespective of the age at death would be turned to be and remain at age thirty. Their virility shall be equal to that of one hundred men.

Mka could hardly believe what Amina was saying. They were entirely different from what the other religious groups he researched on said. He had wanted to ask Amina what would become of female Muslims because Amina did not tell him anything about this. But on a second thought, he restrained himself as he thanked her and changed the topic. Amina was pleased that the topic was changed because most times, because of the level of respect she had for her religion, she always feels uncomfortable discussing it with a non-Muslim. She only had to do the little she had done because it was Mka who was involved. The next thing they discussed was Amina's planned journey to Lagos to meet her parents. That she said would be by the following week. Mka too would be travelling to the East for the long vacation by the same week too.

When Mka got home, he started comparing everything he has known about the promise of paradise by the various religious groups. But in all these, the Christian's seemed to him the authentic one. "But waitoooo, we Christians are even contradicting ourselves over this issue. The Roman Catholics believed that afterlife there is the Purgatory. From where one could escape to the eternal paradise. The Jehovah Witness believed that there is no other Paradise outside this world. The Seventh Day Adventist held that there is no other paradise after death. To them, at death man's soul goes into oblivion. As for the Mormons, their belief was that there would be marriage in paradise. The whole thing is contradicting" soliloquized Mka. He further juxtaposed the Jannah with the Christian's Paradise. He discovered that there were a whole lot of contradiction. Amina has told her that marriage and other sexual activities are major activities in Jannah, but Jesus Christ said that there would be no marrying in the Christian paradise. He also leant from Amina that there were seven levels of Jannah, but the bible did not give a description of the Christian paradise apart from that it is a beautiful city of eternal bliss. At this point, Mka discovered that the religious groups claimed different Paradises with a rigid dogma to back their claims. Then he asked himself "HOW MANY PARADISE DO WE HAVE?". He finally concluded that since most of the religious groups of the world are monotheist in nature, believing in one supreme God, there could be indeed one true God. He also held that that God could be like the proverbial very big elephant that three blind men visited. On getting to the elephant, one of the blind man touched only the leg, the other the trunk, while the other the ears. When the blind men were asked to describe the elephant, they described it based on what each had touched and where very staunch with their individual observations while repulsing the others. Again, Mka concluded that each of these religious groups are bent on where to spend their lives after here. Similarly, God has revealed and given them hope and happiness based on that. So having tested and proven in their various ways that theirs is the ultimate, these whole issues of paradise are both true and false subject to the individual in question.

With all these in mind, Mka decided to toe the lines of Bertrand Russell who held that "the world that I should wish to see would be one free from the virulence of group hostilities and capable of realizing that happiness for all is to be derived rather from co-operation than from strife. I should wish to see a world in which education aimed at mental freedom rather that at imprisoning the minds of the young in a rigid armor of dogma calculated to protect them through life against the shafts of impartial evidence. The world needs open hearts and open minds, and it is not through rigid system, whether old or new, that these can be derived".[1] He decided that he would neither make jest, nor devalue any religious views. One owes what he does not know two things: either to know them or leave and respect them the way they are. As soon as Mka had settled this conviction, it was as if a big burden was taken off him. From that day, he started experiencing joy and relieve he had never had before. He was happy that he had come to a conclusion to his puzzle. It could have been bad for him to travel to the East with such a burdened and confused mind.

---

1   Bertrand vii

By 6:30am on Friday 8th August 2014, he was at Kamuku National Park with Amina. They discussed for about thirty minutes before Amina's bus left for Lagos. By 8am, the bus going to Onitsha was fully loaded, and Mka was on his way to the East for the long vacation.

## CHAPTER NINE

# THE JUDGMENT

**AMINA HAD** met Tolu on Saturday. She went to the Boundary market. Tolu was no longer selling for his senior brother. He had many shops and some apprentices under him. They were very pleased to meet again. They discussed at length. Amina was careful not to mention Mka. Although he had requested that Amina should find out Tolu's way about. Within thirty minutes of their discussion, Tolu narrated to her how Mka had missed her before he left Lagos few years back. Amina who pretended as if she had not heard from Mka since then asked Tolu why they could neither call nor ask for her way about. She pretentiously told Tolu to discontinue telling her about him. "Don't tell me that you have seen someone better than him in the university. The boy truly loves you. We did everything possible to get at you, but it was not possible. He even gave me the assignment of getting your phone contact whenever you come over". As Tolu was still defending Mka, Amina's phone rang. She excused herself to answer the call. The way she was chatting with the caller made Tolu to conclude that there was no longer a place for Mka in Amina's heart. She was probably talking with her lover, Tolu thought. After some minutes of the call, Amina went to Tolu. "Talk with the love of my heart" she said while giving Tolu the phone. Tolu and the phone caller were still exchanging pleasantries while Amina was blushing. She had played a smart game on Tolu who was yet to realize what was going on.

As the phone call was still going on, Amina busted into laughter. The two boys did not know whom they were talking with on phone. Mka had thought that it was Amina's father. Tolu on the other hand had concluded that it was Amina's university lover. "Please give me my phone jaree. See as una dey talk like business partners". Amina collected the phone; put the call on a loudspeaker. She then asked Mka if he knew whom he was talking with. "Is it not your father, as you told me? Mka answered. "My father indeed. So for your dream if you are told that you are talking with my father you go gree, abi?". Asked Amina. "So tell me, who was that? How far, have you met Tolu since you arrived Lagos?" Tolu was surprised to hear his name from the caller. He then interfered "Wait ooo, no be Mka dey talk so".

"OMG! Tolu I am the one. What a surprise. Jess! I could not even recognize your voice. Guess you are now a big boy. Tolu, I really missed you". Interrupted Mka. "This boy. You are a bad boy ooo. How you take enter Amina like this and una no even care to reach me all this while. Una just forget me naa" Said Tolu. The two boys discussed at length without Amina saying anything. She was busy laughing at their conversation. At a point, Amina interrupted "Two dumb friends. Them say two heads are better than one, but no be for where two of you are. See as I jam una two heads, and you could not recognize your voices." "See this Hausa daughter of an Alhaji ooo. For your mind you have played smart on us, right? Taa gbafuo ebea. I knew it was Tolu right from when we started talking. But I wanted you to think that you have succeeded in outsmarting us". Boasted Mka. The conversation lasted for more than three hours. After the call, the three friends were very happy that they could hear one another's voice again. The only thing missing was Mka's physical presence.

From that weekend, Amina began to visit Tolu in his shop regularly. They frequently had conference calls with Mka. The holiday was indeed fun for them. By Monday October 13th, 2014, school resumed. Mka had left Umuagba a week before. He had arranged with Amina and Tolu to come over to Lagos so that they would spend a week together before going back to school. On Sunday 5th, Mka was in Tolu's house. He was very surprised and happy when he saw Tolu's house. He owned a house and a brand new Prado Jeep. That night they discussed far and wide. Mka narrated to him how he got Amina's Facebook username and her other contacts. He also told him how far Amina had helped him starting from when he lost hope of getting admission. The whole story was like a miracle to Tolu who was only happy to know that the two are best of friends. Tolu told his own stories. They were all happy at each other's success stories. "Marry the babe naa." Advised Tolu. "My brother that is what I have in mind ooo" Replied Mka. "But you don tell the girl say you wan marry am" Asked Tolu again. Mka replied negatively. He further expressed his fear. Would both parents allow their children to marry from different ethnic and religious groups? He further told him that he was still a student who was not financially buoyant to marry. "Omo see, that one no be talk. You don see a very beautiful babe wey love you and you love am too. Why are you wasting time? Being a student is not a problem. Propose to her naa." Advised Tolu. After that, they discussed other issues before they went to bed.

The following morning, around 8:00am, Amina visited. Before long, Kehinde joined. Kehinde was Tolu's girlfriend. She was as beautiful as Amina. Although they have been dating for about two years, she never loved Tolu. She was a gold digger who came to make as much fortune as she could from Tolu. After their breakfast, they drove in Tolu's Prado Jeep to Bar-Beach. It was the first time Mka could have such experience. As for Tolu and his girlfriend, it has been a routine. As soon as they got to the beach, they pulled off their dresses leaving on only the swimming kits they were wearing. Mka find it a bit difficult to flow with the game, but he would not like to display how clumsy a university student like him was. Amina on her own side was a bit tensed up. But like Mka, she had to brace up. She undressed her clothes. It was indeed another thing for Mka. He could not believe the youthful hues perching on Amina. She was indeed sexier and sumptuous than Mka had thought. Her breast seemed like a new plant sprouting out from its cotyledon. When she discovered that Mka was admiring her, she became shy and backed him.

Kehinde and Tolu were already lost in the fun. They were kissing and caressing themselves incessantly. Mka was dumfounded when he realized that Tolu was sexing his girlfriend in the beach. He summoned courage, went to Amina who was a few metres away from him. He splashed water on her, and Amina splashed back. It was as if the water washed away their coyness. They went closer to themselves, hugged and kissed. Before long, Mka started fondling her breast as they played. "Wait wait wait, Mka we are going too far. I am getting horny. And I would not want us to do anything funny here, please" Amina said. "It is ok dear. I am sorry, I am getting too far. You are just too beautiful to be resisted. I swear, if you were Portipher's wife, Joseph would not have known it until she is done with him" Mka said.

Amina: Naughty boy. Na today you realized that I am sexy? Is it because I am having mercy on you? Just the shadow of my boobs you saw is making that your cord to be as strong as rod. But wait ooo. Mka the size of you dick is much ooo.

Mka: who told you that you are sexy? I beg let me hear word. It is just that I like mingling with people like you to give them a sense of belonging. You have confirmed that I have a good tool. And you are aware that people like me a rare. Girls want men like me with sizable thing to get them to the peak of their ecstasy.

Amina: Let me hear word joor. If someone sees how you make mouth, he would think that you know what you are saying. But Mka that your thing no get control? Na so it go dey push your pant whenever it sees a shadow of my bra. Don't worry, it is for a while. I will soon get married. By then I will know what you will do. You know I am precious. My husband will enjoy my beauty. He will be the only man to know how sweet I am. So just enjoy the opportunity of feeding yourself with my bra now that you have it.

Mka: (after laughing). Yes my wifey. Mr. Mka will enjoy you to the fullest and you will enjoy him too. He is the right man for you. He has vowed with his life to give you every happiness you deserve. He knows and appreciates your beauty. But Amina, the world knows that you are exceedingly beautiful. I can't wait for the day to come.

It was time to go. The four friends got into Tolu's jeep and drove home. After lunch, the two ladies left. Their next outing was on Friday. That day, it was at Freeman Hotel. Tolu wanted a better one, but Mka preferred there. They went to the bar, had lunch. And went to the various rooms the two men paid for. Amina was surprised when Mka held her hand to a hotel room. It was the same room where the knot of their friendship was tied few years ago, during Amina's birthday party. To her, Mka wanted them to have carnal knowledge of themselves. She was ready. She could do anything for Mka. She was a virgin because Mka was not ready to take her flower. She started to imagine how she would feel as she spread her innocent legs wide and watched Mka's Almighty Anaconda- like creature slowly and ticklishly penetrates her cubicle, breaking the gate of her chambers and then taking her into the ever-exciting world of sexual ecstasy.

When they got to the room, they sat on the mattress. It was not the same mattress they sat some years back. But the colour was the same. Amina was still thinking when Mka realized that she was unease. "Dearie, what is it? You seem unease." Amina replied that nothing was the matter. He then told her that he brought her there for them to discuss themselves. He wanted them to give their relationship a definition before he went back to school. He said "Amina I really want to thank you for everything you have done for me. Knowing you have given my life a definition. Since the day we left this room in 2009, I have never thought of my life without having you as the key player. And I doubt if I can survive without you. Amina, will you marry me?" He said as he knelt down. Tears flowed down Amina's cheeks as she quickly said "Yes, dear. I will marry you" Mka then brought out a diamond ring he had in his pocket, put it on Amina's finger, Kissed her so deeply. Amina was very happy at the proposal. She had been expecting Mka to do that long ago. Although she knew that Mka was not financially buoyant for marriage, she was convinced that he would make a good husband.

After the proposal, Mka reminded her that he would travel back to school the following day. Amina was not happy with that, but there was nothing she could do. She would have loved to go back with him, but that was not possible. The convocation date was not yet fixed and her father would not want her to travel. They discussed many things. After discussing how they would run their family when they get married, Mka brought up the big question. "Will your father approve our marriage?" Amina knew that her father was a hard nut to crack. He also hated to hear that a Muslim and a Christian are dating not to talk of marrying. He was a Muslim bigot and an ethnicist. Amina answered him that as the only daughter, her father loved her so much and would do anything to make her happy. She further added that they would elope if her father refused their marriage.

On the same hand, Mka knew that he had a great work to do in convincing his parents. They would not want any of their children to marry outside the Igbo ethnic group not to talk of a different religious group. But he believed that his own problem might not be as tough as that of Amina's father. Their conclusion was to elope if the parental challenges become difficult to surmount.

When Amina got home that day, her father saw her finger. He was happy to know that his daughter was in a relationship. He pretended not to have seen it. After dinner, Amina told him that someone proposed to marry her. He was very happy. He told her that he could not wait to see his son inlaw. And promised to support the marriage with the best of his ability. After the discussion, she called Mka, told him how happy her father was about the proposal. Mka was delighted to hear that. He asked her if she told him whom the suitor was. Amina replied that it was not yet time to do that. That night, the two lovers were happy. They concluded plans to wed as soon as Mka graduated

By Saturday 13th October, 2014, Mka had gone back to school. As a finalist, he decided to give his studies his full attention. But in NFCS secretariat, Sis Uyime had been a very big challenge for Mka. Knowing that Amina had graduated and that Mka had no other girlfriend in school, she vowed to force herself on Mka. One day, all the members of the fellowship had gone for a convention in Jalingo. It was to last throughout the weekend. Mka had made it open to them that he would not go. So on Wednesday, Sis. Uyime feigned illness. Because of that, she was advised not to join in the convention. As soon as they left, she went to Mka's room, swept and arranged it so beautifully. She placed rose flower and a card written I LOVE YOU SO DEARLY. After that, she hurriedly went to market, bought some fruits and kept for Mka who went to the school library. When he came back around 7:30pm, he saw the way his room was arranged, the flower, the card and the fruits kept carefully for him. He knew that it was Sis. Uyime that did that. As he went to his bookshelf to drop his book, Sis Uyime came in. She was wearing a transparent nightgown. She was not wearing pant and bra. At first, Mka was lost at the sight. As she approached, Mka who did not want to yield to the temptation left the room and could not come back to the secretariat throughout the weekend.

On Friday 19th December, 2014, the school vacated for Christmas break. Mka had agreed with Tolu to come over to Lagos to spend the break. It was then that Amina and Mka agreed to meet her father. Unfortunately, though not surprisingly, Alhaji Mustafa who welcomed Mka thinking that he just visited got angry when he heard that he was his daughter's suitor. He warned Mka not to go close to his daughter again. He promised Amina that he would look for a good Hausa Muslim who would marry her.

Tolu was not happy at that when Mka told him the story of his experience with Amina's father. He encouraged him that he should go ahead with his marriage plan with her. To him, money was not the problem. He offered to finance the wedding and fly them abroad, if the need arose. With the disappointment, the yuletide was not fun for the three friends. Amina's father denied her going out because he knew that Mka was in town.

Because of the disappointment, Mka travelled to the East to complete his break. He told his parents of his plan to marry Amina, but they blatantly refused the marriage on the same reason adduced by Amina's father. It then dawned on Mka that the battle line was drawn. He went back to school on Saturday 3rd, January 2015.

Focusing strictly on his studies, Mka graduated in July 2015 with First Class Honours. He was the best graduating student of the Faculty. As such, he was given scholarship to do his Masters and Doctorate degrees in any university of his choice in any part of the world. He also received gifts of cash and other things. A sum total of Three million, Five Hundred Thousand Naira was given to him. He also received a brand new Toyota Camry and a house in the town of Kaduna. Mka was happy. He planned to use part of the money to pay Amina's bride price. His belief was that having made fame with his academic giantry, Alhaji Mustafa would allow him to marry Amina. But this was not to be. Alhaji never changed his decision. He kept Amina on house arrest. For more than two months, she was kept indoors without a phone so that she could not communicate with Mka. One day, he came home only to see her fuming. She was rushed to the hospital. When her life was resuscitated, she was taken home. She threatened that if she was not given back her cell phone, she would commit suicide. Her father had to give her the phone.

With the phone, the two lovers began to communicate again. Mka was always the one to call. He also sent her airtime everyday. When it was obvious that her father would not support the marriage, he concluded plans with her to elope. He would prepare visa for Amina so that both of them would go to the University of Chicago, where he has chosen to continue his education.

A week before their travelling, Mka called her and told her that everything was ready. They made arrangement with their gateman who would violate Amina father's instruction. Mka earlier promised him the sum of Two Hundred Thousand Naira, if he could let Amina out. Part of the money was given to him while the completion would be the day he would smuggle her out. Amina did not know that her father planted camera in her room. He knew the planned elopement. After their discussion that day, Mka did not call her again. His line was off. Even Tolu who knew all the plans could not reach Mka again. He called Amina, who was surprise to know that Tolu could not hear from Mka too. The conclusion was that Mka had travelled to the United States.

Two days later, the news was everywhere that Mka was murdered and that the security agents were investigating his death. Tolu doubted the news when a friend told him that. He immediately drove out only to find out that all the national dailies had the news on their front pages. He thought of calling Amina. He knew that she would commit suicide if she hears that. He wept bitterly as he vowed to spend the last drop of his blood investigating Mka's death.

That night, he could not sleep. When he finally dozed off, Mka appeared crying. He begged him to go and take Amina home. But Tolu could not understand what he meant. As they were discussing in that trance, Mka said "Alhaji Mustafa sent me somewhere. Go and take Amina to your house, she is waiting for me and I don't know if I would be back soon. Take him to your house so that she won't be tired while waiting for me". As soon as he said that, he disappeared. Tolu woke up and concluded that it was the Alhaji that killed Mka. But he had no corpus delicti in that regard.

The following day, the gateman ran into Amina's room. He was shading tears as he said "Small madam, wallai I dey sorry for what I happen to my husband. I saw this newspaper this morning and I cry. As I don die, I no go give me the money wey remain abi? Wallai, I dey sorry for me." After saying this, he wanted to leave, but Amina called him back. Collected the newspaper from him, gazed at it and slumped. The gateman called her, but she could not answer. He raced downstairs and phoned the Alhaji. Within five minutes, he drove in and saw her daughter unconscious. Besides her was a newspaper containing the story of Mka's death. There was no time for questioning. He drove her to hospital. Amina was unconscious for one month. And Tolu had been trying her line but her phone was off.

One day, he summoned courage and went to Amina's house. The gateman broke the sad news of Amina's condition. He drove straight to the hospital because he knew their family doctor. Both the doctor and Alhaji Mustafa were there when he rushed in. Nobody uttered a word. He went straight to the bed and said "Amina no, no, no. You cannot do this. You are the only person I now have in this entire world. Amina no." Before he could finish the statement, Amina who had not made any move for the past one month opened her eyes. Tears rolled down her cheek. The doctor and her father were happy. From that day, she started responding to treatment. But she was yet to utter any word. After a week, she seemed fully recovered from the unconsciousness. But her behavior was abnormal. It was later discovered that when she slumped, she hit her head on the floor which touched her brain.

After two months, Amina was brought back home. But she was then mentally unstable. The only thing she could say within intervals was "Mka".

The investigation into the murder of Mka knew no success. There was no trace of how he died. One day, Tolu visited Amina who was alone in her room. He gave him some things he bought for her. They stayed for more than an hour without anyone saying anything. It was only "Mka" that came out within intervals from Amina's mouth. Tolu stood up, bade Amina goodbye but as he wanted to leave, she pleaded through miming for him to sit. Amina took a piece of paper and wrote "Why are you a coward? You claim to be Mka's best friend but you don't want to fight his course. Please if you cannot tell the world that my father killed our friend, don't visit me again". Tolu was surprise. He wondered how Amina knew about what she wrote. She was also stunned to know that Amina could write something reasonable. He then said, "I will do that. Bye". And left.

The following day, he travelled to Kaduna State police headquarters and reported that he knew who murdered Mka. He narrated how Amina and Mka wanted to elope. He further offered to sponsor the investigation. The case was then reopened as investigation continued with all vigour. The first place the police and Tolu went to was Mka's apartment. It was locked since the investigation was going on. They searched everywhere without seeing both Mka and Amina's international passports. They went to the ABU but got no information there. They concluded to drive to Lagos the following day. On getting to Alhaji Mustafa's house, he was about to drive out. They showed him their search warrants. He allowed them to search his house. After a thorough search, there was nothing to show that he had a connection with Mka's death. They went to Amina's room. Searched thoroughly. There was no exhibit there too.

When they left, Tolu who knew that Alhaji Mustafa would become suspicion of his involvement in the investigation curtailed his movement for his safety. He invited the Alhaji's gateman. He promised to give him anything if he could tell him all he knew about Mka's murder. The gateman told him that he knew nothing apart from the fact that he saw the picture of his dead body on his boss's television a night before the news of Mka's death circulated. On hearing this, Tolu gave the gateman Five Thousand Naira. And pleaded with him to go to the police station with him. He promised to give him more money if he could tell the police exactly what he told him. At the police station, the gateman repeated the same thing he told Tolu. The police officer asked him if he was watching the television with the Alhaji. He said no, rather two men that visited his boss. He explained that he went to the sitting room that night to give the Alhaji a recharge card he sent him to buy. As soon as he entered, he glanced at the television and what he saw was a corpse with a face that looked like Mka. Immediately, his boss scolded him to hand him over the card and go to his duty post. The police asked him if he knew any of those his boss's friends who were watching the television with him. He answered negatively, though he assured the police that he would recognize them if he sees them. The policeman brought out his international passport, asked him if he has seen his boss with such thing since Mka died. He replied that the only day he saw such thing was that same night his boss was watching the television with his friends. He said that they were two in number though they were not his boss's own, rather one of the two men with his boss was the one holding them. The police thanked the gateman and threaten that if he disclose to his boss of their interrogation with him, they would arrest and kill him. Tolu drove the gateman home. Alhaji Mustafa was not around. So he went in and instructed Amina to be sensitive of any movement in their compound. He knew that Amina could hear and understand very well, but her problem was to speak. He gave the gateman another Five Thousand Naira and promise to give him more if he would cooperate with him in subsequent time. He further told him to report any strange movement in the house to Amina. The gateman was happy to make such a sum that day.

Alhaji Mustafa sensed danger. He started sensing that Tolu and the policemen were suspecting him. That night, he invited Hitler. Hitler was a very hefty and notorious man in Ajengule, Lagos. He was one of the men the gateman described to the police as his boss's friend. When Hitler entered, the gateman went and notified Amina of his presence in the house and left. She went and stood on the balcony. Before long, Hitler left the compound. Amina was able to recognize him.

The following day, at around 10:00am, Tolu saw Alhaji Mustafa in the Boundary Market. He rushed to his house to give Amina what he bought for her. As he wanted to leave, Amina gave her a scrap of paper where she wrote "Hitler came to my house last night. He was with my father". Tolu immediately took the paper and hurried out to the gate. He asked the gateman if anyone visited the Alhaji the previous night. He said "na the same man wey watch the television with my boss the night wey Oga Mka I die. Na him get that type of book wey oga police showed me" Tolu gave him another Five Thousand Naira and promised him more.

He went to the police and told them everything he heard. Immediately, the police drove to Hitler's house. They searched everywhere. They did not see anything that related to what they were looking for. As soon as they wanted to leave, there was power supply and Hitler's television displayed Mka's apartment in Kaduna. Hitler immediately turned off the television set. The police did not understand what happened. They were not the same people that went to Mka's house in

Kaduna. They told Hitler that he was a suspect of a murder case. Therefore, he would go with them to the police station for interrogation. Hitler objected that they should go while he would come later, but they refused. He decided to follow them. But before that, he ejected a memory card that was on his DVD Player and wanted to destroy it. The police immediately intervened but he quickly swallowed it.

When they got to the police station, Hitler was asked to make his statement. The policeman who apprehended him contacted both Tolu and the Kaduna State police division. He also narrated the scene he saw on Hitler's television and how he wanted to destroy the memory card. Tolu drove him to Mka's apartment in Kaduna for further investigation. He was stunned to see that the scene he saw on the television was Mka's bedroom. He phoned the Lagos State division to keep Hitler on a strict surveillance. He instructed them to make sure that he did not excrete in the toilet. When they drove to Lagos, they interrogated him further, but he blatantly refused knowing what they were saying. The police then decided to wait till he excretes the memory card. But for the two weeks Hitler was in detention, he could not defecate. He also refused to eat anything.

To Ahaji Mustafa, the investigation was over because for the past two weeks, there was nothing to show that. Besides, he has confiscated everything relating to the murder of Mka. The last memory card was the one he paid Hitler the last time they met to destroy. He was not aware that Hitler was under detention for the past two weeks. To his greatest bewilderment, the following day, it was on air that Hitler was under detention for allegedly murdering Mka. The case was charged to court. For the next one month that followed, all allegations against Hitler were with no tangible evidence to back it up.

The case was to be ruled on Friday 4th December, 2015. Before then, Hitler who refused to eat for the past seven weeks he was under detention was sick. He has not defecated since then too. On Thursday, 3rd, he was critically ill and was rushed to the hospital. When he recovered from his unconsciousness, he was very hungry and had to eat. After the meal, he went to the lavatories, defecated, took his bath and was kept under police custody for the following day when he would be justified of his allegation.

The whole court room was filled to the brim. Everyone was convinced that Hitler could not be proven guilty by the prosecuting council. As soon as the Judge wanted to pronounce his judgment, the council pleaded for objection which was granted to him. He told the court that he wanted to show them his last exhibit. He brought out a memory card, asked the court clerk to play the content. Everyone was surprise to see how Hitler and Jimmy murdered Mka. The memory card was gotten from Hitler's excreta the previous day. The prosecuting council payed the doctor to do everything possible for

Hitler to ease himself at least thrice before the judgement day. The excreta, he said should be collected with poo and given to him. The doctor did exactly that. During his unconscious state, Hitler excreted unknowingly. It was from there that the memory card was gotten.

As soon as the court saw the scene where this was done, the case changed. When Hitler was further interrogated, he confessed how he was paid with Jimmy by Alhaji Mustafa to go and murder Mka. The Alhaji and Jimmy who came to the court to celebrate with Hitler were apprehended. Before they could be sentenced to death, the Prosecuting council pleaded for another objection. He said he had a surprise for the court. He clapped his hands and Mka and Tolu came out from the rear door. The whole courtroom was thrown into confusion. People could not believe that Mka was still alive. He narrated how two men came to his house and shot him after collecting his international passport and that of Amina. According to him the next place he saw himself after the shooting was in Sis Uyime friend's house. Sis. Uyime narrated to him how she saw her lying helplessly the night he was shot and took him to her friend, Esosa's house. Sis Uyime and Esosa were final year medical students of the ABU. She had told Esosa how much she loved Mka before the shooting incident occurred. So when she saw Mka that night, she phoned Esosa who had a car. She drove them to her house where both of them practiced what they had learnt on Mka. When Mka got better, Sis.Uyime told him how she picked him up. She convinced him to dress and disguise himself as a woman and they traveled to Sis. Uyime's house in Akwa-Ibom State of South Southern Nigeria with her. Sis, Uyime and Mka were following the news of the investigation. Though they decided not to show up. Even when they wanted to open up, there was nobody Mka could remember their phone contact. On the 2nd of December, Sis. Uyime who had told her father everything about Mka pleaded with him to drive them to Lagos.

Luckily, when they got to a police station closer to the court where the judgment would be passed, Tolu and his lawyer were leaving the station. He was the first to see Mka. He was stunned as he could not believe what he saw. He wanted to run away but his lawyer asked him what the problem was. When he told him, the lawyer went to them and said, "you look like my friend, Odu" Mka replied that he was Mka Odu. The lawyer then signaled Tolu to come. The two friends recognized and hugged themselves. The lawyer immediately asked them to enter the car. They drove to Tolu's house where Mka and Sis. Uyime narrated everything that happened. They were then told to be ready to go to the court on 4th.

Mka was put to the duck, after narrating his story, the judge sentenced Alhaji Mustafa, Hitler and Jimmy to death by hanging.

The following day, Mka went to the Alhaji's house. He was surprised to see Amina looking shabby like a mad woman. Amina was overwhelmed when she saw him. She screamed his name, ran to him, and hugged him. Everyone was surprise that Amina then started talking. She told them that she could talk all this while. But she vowed that she would not. The only thing she would be saying till when she would dye would be Mka's name.

Within a month, Mka and Amina got married. Tolu was there Best-man while Sis. Uyime was the chief bridesmaid. On Mka's wedding day, Tolu and Sis. Uyime fell deeply in love. Within a short while, they got married.

After their wedding, Mka and his wife travelled to the United States to continue with their educations.

# GLOSSARY OF SOME SELECTED WORDS

| | |
|---|---|
| **Dibia** | Herbalist |
| **Nzu** | White mood, clay sand. |
| **Omu** | Palm fronds |
| **Ijenwangbada** | A traditional bead made from palm fronds |
| **Abubu** | A fibrous wood made from a processed palm fruit that causes much smoke. |
| **Eze-amadioha** | An Amadioha chief priest. |
| **Umunna** | kinsmen. |
| **Omenala** | tradition. |
| **Iwa-akwa** | Initiation ceremony used to initiate one into manhood. |
| **Obiama** | village hall. |
| **Oku** | A natively made bowl. |
| **Oji** | Kola nut |
| **Mkpo-nala** | Canon shot |

| | |
|---|---|
| **JSCE** | Junior Secondary Certificate Exam. |
| **Amadioha** | Deity. |
| **Page six** | |
| **Ndi ogo** | In laws |
| **Ogugu** | palm branches |
| **Eze** | king |
| **Ugba** | Oil beam |
| **Ukwu-ewu** | Goat leg |
| **Afo** | An Igbo traditional market day. |
| **Juo-ogu** | Pour Libation. |
| **Odighinkemjuru** | Someone that accepts everything and never rejecting any. |
| **Nkpo** | A locally made structure in a kitchen where food and utensils are kept. |
| **Ude-aki** | A local cream prepared by roasting palm kernel. |
| **Oro-oro** | A hide and seek game. |
| **Oga** | Agame that involves clapping of hands in a particular rhythm, while the feet do the actual game. |
| **Akwukwo awolowo** | The independent leave. |

| | |
|---|---|
| **Engli-Igbo** | A mixture of both the English and the Igbo languages. |
| **Agu** | Lion |
| **Ikpo** | A bell like structure hung on hunting dogs' necks that catalyze them to action. |
| **Oja** | A traditional flute. |
| **Opi** | Whistle |
| **Ndi-nta** | Hunters |
| **Ediabali** | Wolf. |
| **Ikoro** | Locally made gong. |
| **Kpukpukpu-gele** | A typical moonlight play. |
| **Mmum Mbele** | Snail hunting exercise done at night. |
| **Okporama** | Playground. |
| **Vein** | Male's genital organ |
| **Oyibo** | White/Englishman |
| **Oru-Ogige** | Church compound cleaning. |
| **UTME** | Universal Tertiary Education Board |
| **UNN** | University of Nigeria, Nsukka. |
| **ABU** | Almadu Bello Univeristy |
| **JAMB** | Joint Admission and MATRICULATION Board. |

| | |
|---|---|
| **NECO** | Nnational Examination Council |
| **SSCE** | Senior Secondary Certificate Examination |
| **Akuko-ifo** | Folklore |
| **Ajuala** | Viper |
| **Nkita** | dog. |
| **Mbele** | Snail |
| **Omo** | A Yoruba word for a young man. |
| **Eeman** | Faith |
| **Keke-Napep** | Tricycle. |
| **Oya Now** | Let us start/begin |
| **Ewa-agonyi** | A typical porridge beans cooked in Yorubaland |
| **Ugu** | Fluted pumpkin leaf |
| **JJC** | Journey Just Come. An amateur or inexperienced person in a particular thing. |
| **Ndi Ofe-Mmanu** | A derogatory term used by the Igbos to refer to the Yorubas. Ofe is soup, while Mmanu is oil. It was said that the Yorubas would always cook soup filled with red oil; as such, they were thus known for that. |
| **PCC** | Parochial Church Committee |

**church's pawpaw**    Having sex with ones female church member

**Okwala ya**    She has missed it. She has been denied of it.